The Life and Adventures of Joaquín Murieta

The Life and Adventures of Joaquín Murieta

John Rollin Ridge

MINT EDITIONS

The Life and Adventures of Joaquín Murieta was first published in 1854.

This edition published by Mint Editions 2021.

ISBN 9781513283418 | E-ISBN 9781513288437

Published by Mint Editions®

minteditionbooks.com

Publishing Director: Jennifer Newens
Design & Production: Rachel Lopez Metzger
Project Manager: Micaela Clark
Typesetting: Westchester Publishing Services

Contents

Preface

The following production, aside from its intrinsic merit, will, no doubt, be read with increased interest when it is known that the author is a "Cherokee Indian," born in the woods—reared in the midst of the wildest scenery—and familiar with all that is thrilling, fearful, and tragical in a forest-life. His own experiences would seem to have well fitted him to portray in living colors the fearful scenes which are described in this book, connected as he was, from the age of seventeen up to twenty three, with the tragical events which occurred so frequently in his own country, the rising of factions, the stormy controversies with the whites, the fall of distinguished chiefs, family feuds, individual retaliation and revenge, and all the consequences of that terrible civil commotion which followed the removal of the Cherokee Nation from the east to the west of the Mississippi, under the administration of Gen. Jackson.

When a small boy, he saw his father (the celebrated chief and orator, known among the Indians by the name of "Sca-lee-los-kee") stabbed to death by a band of assassins employed by a political faction, in the presence of his wife and children at his own home. While the bleeding corpse of his father was yet lying in the house, surrounded by his weeping family, the news came that his grandfather, a distinguished old war chief, was also killed, and, fast upon this report, that others of his near relatives were slain. His mother, a white woman and a native of Connecticut, fled from the bloody precincts of the nation, with her children, and sought refuge in the United States.

Her oldest son, "Yellow Bird," after remaining several years among the whites, returned to his own country and asserted the rights of his family, which had been prostrated since the death of his father. He was intimately concerned for several years in the dangerous contentions which made the Cherokee Nation a place of blood; and, finally, not succeeding in overthrowing the murderers of his father and the oppressors of his country, who were then in power, and, having furnished them with a pretext for putting him out of the way by killing a prominent member of their party, he left his country once more and, in 1850, came to the State of California. So far, we know his history. Whether he will ever meet with success in his purposes with regard to his own people, we cannot say, but we hope that he will.

The perusal of this work will give those who are disposed to be curious an opportunity to estimate the character of Indian talent. The aboriginal race has produced great warriors, and powerful orators, but literary men—only a few.

Editor's Preface

The author, in presenting this book to the public, is aware that its chief merit consists in the reliability of the ground work upon which it stands and not in the beauty of its composition. He has aimed to do a service—in his humble way—to those who shall hereafter inquire into the early history of California, by preserving, in however rude a shape, a record of at least a portion of those events which have made the early settlement of this State a living romance through all time.

Besides, it is but doing justice to a people who have so far degenerated as to have been called by many, "A Nation of Cowards," to hold up a manifest contradiction, or at least an exception to so sweeping an opinion, in the character of a man who, bad though he was, possessed a soul as full of unconquerable courage as ever belonged to a human being. Although the Mexicans may be whipped by every other nation, in a battle of two or five to one, yet no man who speaks the truth can ever deny that there lived one Mexican whose nerves were as iron in the face of danger and death.

The author has not thrown this work out into the world recklessly, or without authority for his assertions in the main, it will be found to be strictly true. Where he has mentioned localities as being the harboring places of Joaquin, he has meant invariably to say that persons *then* connected (at the date of the events narrated) with those localities stood in the doubtful position in which he has placed them.

I

His Boyhood, Early Education, And Personal Appearance—His Acquaintance With Americans In Mexico—His Winning of the Beautiful Rosita—His Arrival in California—His Honest Occupation As a Miner—His Domicil Intruded Upon By Lawless Men—Their Outrages Upon Him and His Mistress—His Removal to a New Locality—New Intrusions and Oppressions

Sitting down, as I now do, to give to the public such events of the life of Joaquín Murieta as have come into my possession, I am moved by no desire to administer to any depraved taste for the dark and horrible inhuman action, but rather by a wish to contribute my might to those materials out of which the early history of California shall be composed. Aside from the interest naturally excited by the career of a man so remarkable in the annals of crime—for in deeds of daring and blood he has never been exceeded by any of the renowned robbers of the Old or New World who have preceded him—his character is well worth the scrutiny of the intelligent reader as being a product of the social and moral condition of the country in which he lived, while his individual record becomes a part of the most valuable, because it is a part of the earliest history of the State.

We must here premise that there existed another Joaquin, contemporaneously with the subject of this narrative, who bore the several titles of O'Comorenia, Valenzuela, Botellier and Carillo. His true surname was Valenzuela, and he was a distinguished subordinate of Joaquín Murieta. He used, however, by many persons to be mistaken for his chief; and certain individuals who knew him simply as "Joaquin," and who saw him after the announcement of Murieta's death, insisted with great pertinacity that the terrible bandit was still alive.

Joaquín Murieta was a Mexican of good blood, borne in the province of Sonora, of respectable parents, and educated to a degree sufficient for the common purposes of life in the schools of his native country. While growing up, he was remarkable for a very mild and peaceable disposition, and gave no sign of that indomitable and daring spirit which afterwards characterized him. Those who knew him in his school-boy days speak affectionately of his generous and noble nature at that period of his life, and can scarcely credit the fact, that the renowned and bloody bandit of California was one and the same being.

The first considerable interruption in the general smooth current of his existence, occurred in the latter portion of his seventeenth year. Near the rancho of his father resided a "packer," one Feliz, who, as ugly as sin itself, had a daughter named Rosita. Her mother was dead, and she, although but sixteen, was burdened with the responsibility of a house-keeper in their simple home, for her father and a younger brother, whose name will hereafter occasionally occur in the progress of this narration.

Rosita, though in humble circumstances, was of Castilian descent, and showed her superior origin in the native royalty of her look and general dignity of her bearing. Yet she was of that voluptuous order to which so many of the dark-eyed daughters of Spain belong, and the rich blood of her race mounted to cheeks, lips and eyes. Her father doted upon and was proud of her, and it was his greatest happiness, on returning from occasional packing expeditions through the mountains of Sonora (he was simply employed by a more wealthy individual) to receive the gentle ministries of his gay and smiling daughter.

Joaquin having nothing to do but ride his father's horses, and give a general superintendence to the herding of stock upon the rancho, was frequently a transient caller at the cabin of Feliz, more particularly when the old man was absent, making excuses for a drink of water or some such matter, and prolonging his stay for the purpose of an agreeable chit-chat with the by no means backward damsel. She had read of bright and handsome lovers, in the stray romances of the day, and well interpreted, no doubt, the mutual emotions of loving hearts.

Indeed Nature herself is a sufficient instructor, without the aid of books, where tropic fire is in the veins, and lowing health runs hand in hand with the imagination. It was no wonder, then, that the youthful Joaquin and the precocious and blooming Rosita, in the absence, on each side, of all other like objects of attraction, should begin to feel the presence of each other as a necessity. They loved warmly and passionately. The packer being absent more than half the time, there was every opportunity for the youthful pair to meet, and their intercourse was, with the exception of the occasional intrusion of her brother Reyes, a mere boy, absolutely without restraint. Rosita was one of those beings who yield all for love, and, ere, she took time to consider of her duties to society, to herself, or to her father, she found herself in the situation of a mere mistress to Joaquin.

Old Feliz broke in at last, upon their felicity, by a chance discovery. Coming home one day from a protracted tour in the mountains, he found no one in the cabin but his son Reyes, who told him that Rosita and Joaquin had gone out together on the path leading up the little stream that ran past the dwelling. Following up the path indicated, the old man came upon the pair, in a position, as Byron has it in the most diabolical of his works, "loving, natural and Greek." His rage knew no bounds, but Joaquin did not tarry for its effects. On the contrary, he fled precipitately from the scene. Whether he showed a proper regard for the fair Rosita in so doing, it is not our province to discuss.

All we have to do is to state what occurred, and leave moral discrepancies to be harmonized as they best may. At any rate, the loving girl never blamed him for his conduct, for she took the earliest opportunity of a moonlight night, to seek him at his father's rancho, and throw herself into his arms.

About this time, Joaquin had received a letter from a half-brother of his, who had been a short time in California, advising him by all means to hasten, to that region of romantic adventure and golden reward. He was not long in preparing for the trip. Mounted upon a valuable horse, with his mistress by his side upon another, and with a couple of packed mules before him, laden with provisions and necessaries, he started for the fields of gold. His journey was attended with no serious difficulties, and the trip was made with expedition.

The first that we hear of him in the Golden State is that in the spring of 1850, he is engaged in the honest occupation of a miner in the Stanislaus placers, then reckoned among the richest portions of the mines. He was then eighteen years of age, a little over the medium height, slenderly but gracefully built, and active as a young tiger.

His complexion was neither very dark nor very light, but clear and brilliant, and his countenance is pronounced to have been at that time, exceedingly handsome and attractive. His large black eyes kindling with the enthusiasm of his earnest nature, his firm and well-formed mouth, his well-shaped head, from which the long, glossy black hair hung down over his shoulders, his silvery voice, full of generous utterance, and the frank and cordial manner which distinguished him, made him beloved by all with whom he came in contact. He had the confidence and respect of the whole community around him, and was fast amassing a fortune in his rich mining claim. He had built him a comfortable mining residence, in which he had domiciled his heart's treasure—the beautiful girl whom we have described.

The country then was full of careless and desperate men, who bore the name of Americans, but failed to support the honor and the dignity of that title. A feeling was prevalent among this class, of contempt for any and all Mexicans, whom they looked upon as, conquered subjects of the United States, having no rights which could stand before a haughtier and superior race. They made no exceptions. If the proud blood of the Castilian mounted to the cheek of a partial descendant of the Mexiques, showing that he had inherited the old chivalrous spirit of his Spanish ancestry, they looked upon it as a saucy presumption in one so inferior to them. The prejudice of color, the antipathy of races, which are always stronger and bitterer with the ignorant and unlettered, they could not overcome, or if they could, would not, because it afforded them a convenient excuse for their unmanly cruelty and oppression.

One pleasant evening, as Joaquin was sitting in his doorway, after a hard day's work, gazing forth upon the sparkling waters of the Stanislaus River, and listening to the musical voice of Rosita, who was singing a dreamy ditty of her native land, a band of the lawless men above alluded to approached the house and accosted its owner in a very insulting and supercilious manner, asking him by what means he, a d—d Mexican, presumed to be working a mining claim on American ground. Joaquin, who spoke very good English, having often met with Americans in Sonora, replied that, under the treaty of Guadalupe Hidalgo, he had a right to become a citizen of the United States, and that as such he considered himself.

"Well, sir," said one of the party, "we allow no Mexicans to work in this region, and you have got to leave this claim."

As might have been expected, the young Mexican indignantly remonstrated against such an outrage. He had learned to believe that to be an American was to be the soul of honor and magnanimity, and he could hardly realize that such a piece of meanness and injustice could be perpetrated by any portion of a race whom he had been led so highly to respect. His remonstrances only produced additional insult and insolence, and finally a huge fellow stepped forward and struck him violently in the face.

Joaquin, with an explosion of rage, sprang toward his bowie-knife, which lay on the bed near by where he had carelessly thrown it on his arrival from work, when his affrighted mistress, fearing that his rashness, in the presence of such an overpowering force might be fatal to him, frantically seized and held him. At this moment his assailant again advanced, and, rudely throwing the young woman aside, dealt him a succession of blows which soon felled him, bruised and bleeding, to the floor.

Rosita, at this cruel outrage, suddenly seemed transformed into a being of a different nature, and herself seizing the knife, she made a vengeful thrust at the American. There was fury in her eye and vengeance in her spring, but what could a tender female accomplish, against such ruffians? She was seized by her tender wrists, easily disarmed, and thrown fainting and helpless upon the bed. Meantime Joaquin had been bound hand and foot, by others of the party, and, lying in that condition he saw the cherished companion of his bosom deliberately violated by these very superior specimens of the much vaunted Anglo-Saxon race.

Leaving him in his agony, they gave him to understand that, if he was found in that cabin, or upon his claim after the expiration of the next ten days, they would take his life. The soul of the young man was from that moment darkened, and, as he himself related afterwards, he swore, with clenched hands, as his mistress unbound him, that he would live for revenge. She, weeping, implored him to live for *her*, as he knew she only lived for *him*, and try to forget in some other and happier scene the bitter misery of the present. He was prevailed upon by her kindness and her tears, and soon after the young couple took their departure for a more northern portion of the mines.

The next we hear of them, they are located on a nice little farm on the banks of a beautiful stream that watered a fertile valley far out in the seclusion of the mountains of Calaveras. Here the somewhat saddened adventurer deemed that he might hope for peace and again be happy. But it was not so destined. One day, as he was engaged with axe and mattock in clearing his ground, several Americans rode up to the fencing of his little retreat, and notified him that they allowed no infernal Mexican intruders, like him, to own land in that section. Joaquin's blood boiled in his veins, but he answered mildly that the valley was unoccupied save by himself, that lie acknowledged allegiance to the American Government, that the treaty of peace between the

United States and Mexico gave him his choice of citizenship either in California or in Mexico as he liked, that he had been already driven from the mines without any crime or offence on his part, and all he now asked was a very small patch of ground and the shelter of a humble home for himself and "wife."

He was peremptorily told to leave, and, we blush to say it, compelled to abandon the spot he had selected and the fruits of his labor.

It is honorable to him to say that his spirit was still unbroken, nor had the iron so far entered his soul as to sear up the innate sensitiveness to honor and right which reigned in his bosom. Twice ruined in his honest pursuit of fortune, he resolved still to labor on with unflinching brow and with that true moral bravery which throws its redeeming light forward upon all his subsequently dark and criminal career. How deep must have been the anguish of that young heart, and how strongly rooted the native honesty of his soul, none can know or imagine but they that have been tried in like manner.

He bundled up his little moveable property, and again started forth to strike once more, like a' brave and honest man, for fortune and for happiness. He arrived at Murphy's Diggings, in Calaveras County, in the month of April, 1850, and went again to mining, this time without interruption; but meeting with nothing like his former success, he soon abandoned that business, and devoted his time to dealing "monte," a game which is common in Mexico, and had been almost universally adopted by gamblers in Mexico. It is considered by the Mexican in no manner a disreputable employment, and many well-reared young men from the Atlantic States have resorted to it, in time past, as a "profession" in this land of luck and chances. It was once in much better odor than it is now, although it is at present a game which may be played on very fair and honest principles, provided anything can be strictly honest or fair which allows the taking of money without a valuable consideration in return.

It was therefore looked upon as no departure from rectitude on the part of Joaquin, when hoe commenced the dealing of "monte." Having a very pleasing exterior and being, despite of all his sorrows, very gay and lively in his disposition, lie attracted many persons to his table, and won their money with such skill and grace, or lost his own with such perfect good humor, that he was considered by all the very beau ideal of a gambler and the prince of clever fellows. His sky seemed clear and his prospects bright, but Fate was weaving her mysterious web around him, and 'fitting him by the force of circumstances to become what nature never intended le should be.

His half brother, of whom we have spoken, resided on a small tract of land in the vicinity of Murphy's Diggings. Joaquin had paid him a visit, and returned to the Diggings on a horse borrowed from his brother. The animal, which his brother had bought and paid his money for, proved to have been originally stolen, and being recognized by a number of individuals in town, as well as by the owner, a stout rough-grained man, named J—s, an excitement was raised on the subject. Joaquin suddenly found himself surrounded by a furious mob, many of them strangers to him, who were by no means sparing of their threats and insults.

"So my covey," said J—s, laying his hand on Joaquin's shoulder, "you are the chap that's been a stealing horses and mules around here, for the last six months, are you?"

"You charge me unjustly," replied Joaquin. "I borrowed this horse of my half brother who bought it from an American, which he can easily prove, as well as show a bill of sale besides."

"This is all gammon," said J—s, "and you are nothing but a dirty thief."

"Hang him!" "Hang him!" cried out several voices from the crowd, and the young Mexican was at once seized and bound. Some one, more moderate than the rest, suggested that it would be better, before proceeding to extremities, to see what the half brother had to say for himself.

"Yes, nab him too!" exclaimed various persons in the mob, and they at once started for the half brother's house, taking their prisoner along with them.

"All I want you to do, gentlemen," said Joaquin, "is to give my brother a chance to prove his and my innocence, Let him have time to summon his witnesses."

This remark was only answered with jeers and contempt. Arriving at the place sought for, the brother of Joaquin being readily found, he was seized, with scarcely a word of explanation, hurried to a tree and swung by the neck, amid the hootings of the mob, until he was dead. Joaquin shed tears of agony at the sight, and begged that they would proceed at once to deal out the same fate to him. But the original intention, with regard to him, was changed by some sudden revulsion of feeling in the crowd, and a far more humiliating punishment inflicted.

The unhappy young man was bound to the same tree upon which the lifeless form of his brother was swinging, and publicly disgraced with the lash. An eye-witness of this scene declared to the author that he never saw such an expression in all his life as at this moment passed over the face of Joaquin. He cast a look of unutterable scorn and scowling hate upon his torturers, and measured them from head to foot, as though he would imprint their likenesses upon his memory forever. In grim silence he received their blows, disdaining to utter a groan. The deed being over and his hands unbound, he resumed the garb which had been stripped from his shoulders, and was left alone with his dead brother.

Who can tell the piercing grief of his now desolate heart, and the tempest of mingled wrath and woe which swept over him as he lowered the dead form of his brother, and, with the few friends who came to his assistance, proceeded to pay him the last sad rites of rude and humble sepulture? Standing over the grave of his last and dearest relative, he swore an oath of the most awful solemnity, that his soul should never know peace until his hands were dyed deep in the blood of his enemies! Fearfully did he keep that oath, as the following pages will show.

II

A Change in Joaquin's Character—Mysterious Disappearances—Murders Upon the Highway—An Organized Banditti—Ranches Lose Their Stock—The Killing of the Deputy Sheriff of Santa Clara County—Encounter With the Bandits By the Sheriff of Yuba County

A change came over the character of Joaquin, suddenly and irrevocably. Wanton cruelty and the tyranny of prejudice had reached their climax. The soul of the injured, man grew dark, and the barriers of honor, rocked into atoms by the strong passions which shook his heart like an earthquake, crumbled around him. He was no more the genial, generous, open-hearted Murieta, as of yore. He walked apart in moody silence, avoided all intercourse with Americans and was seen to ride off into the mountains in company with such of his countrymen as he had never before condescended to be associated with.

It was not long before an American was found dead in the vicinity of Murphy's Diggings, having been almost literally cut to pieces with a knife. Although horribly mangled, he was recognized as one of the mob engaged in the whipping of Joaquin and the hanging of his brother.

A doctor, passing in the neighborhood of this murder, was met shortly afterward, by two men on horseback, who fired their revolvers at him, but, owing to his speed on foot, and the unevenness of the ground, he succeeded in escaping with no further injury than having a bullet shot through his hat, within an inch of the top of his head! A panic spread among the rash individuals who had composed that mob, and they were afraid to stir out on their ordinary business.

Whenever any one of them strayed out of sight of his camp, or ventured to travel on the highway, he was shot down suddenly and mysteriously. Report after report came, into the villages that Americans had been found dead on the highways, having been either shot or stabbed, and it was invariably discovered for many weeks, that the murdered men belonged to the mob who had outraged Joaquin. It was fearful and it was strange, to see how swiftly and mysteriously those men disappeared. J—s, the owner of the horse which had been the occasion of the mob, was among the missing, but whether he slid off for distant parts, in fear of his life, or fell a victim to the wrath of the avenger, I have never learned. Certain it is that Murieta's revenge was very nearly complete. Said an eye witness of these events, (an acquaintance of mine, named Burns,) in reply to an inquiry—which I addressed him:

"I am inclined to think Joaquin *wiped out* the most of those prominently engaged in whipping him."

Thus far, who can blame him? But the iron had entered too deeply into his soul for him to stop here. He had contracted a hatred for the whole American race, and was determined to shed their blood, whenever and wherever an opportunity occurred. It was no time now for him to retrace his steps. He had committed deeds which made him amenable to the law, and his only safety lay in a persistence in the unlawful course which he had begun. It was necessary that he should have horses, and that he should have money. These he could not obtain except by robbery and murder, and thus he became an outlaw and a bandit on the verge of his nineteenth year.

The year 1850 rolled away, marked with the eventful history of the young man's wrongs and trials, his bitter revenge on those who had perpetrated the crowning act of his deep injury and disgrace; and, as it closed, it shut him away forever from his peace of mind and purity of heart. He walked forth into the future a dark, determined criminal, and all his proud nobility of soul, save in fitful gleams, existed only in memory.

In 1851 it became generally known that an organized banditti were ranging the country; but it was not yet ascertained who was the leader. Travelers, laden with the produce of the mines, were met upon the roads by well dressed men who politely requested them to "stand and deliver;" persons riding alone in the many wild and lonesome regions, which form a large portion of this country, were skillfully noosed with the lasso (which the Mexicans throw with great accuracy, being able thus to capture wild cattle, elk, and sometimes even grizzly bears, upon the plains,) dragged from their saddles and murdered in the adjacent thickets. Horses of the finest mettle were stolen from the ranches, and, being tracked up, were found in the possession of a determined band of men, ready to retain them at all hazards, and fully able to stand their ground.

The scenes of murder and robbery shifted with the rapidity of lightning. At one time the northern counties would be suffering slaughters and depredations, at another the southern, and, before one would have imagined it possible, the east and the west and every point of the compass would be in trouble. There had been before this, neither in 1849 nor in 1850, any such thing as an organized banditti, and it had been a matter of surprise to every one, since the country was so well adapted to a business of this kind—the houses scattered at such distances along the roads, the plains so level and open in which to ride with speed, and the mountains so rugged with their ten thousand fastnesses, in which to hide! Grass was abundant in the far-off valleys which lay hidden in the rocky gorges, cool, delicious streams made music at the feet of the towering peals, or came leaping down, in gladness from their sides—game abounded on every hand, and nine unclouded months of the year made a climate so salubrious that nothing could be sweeter than a day's rest under the tall pines, or a night's repose under the open canopy of heaven.

Joaquin knew his advantages. His superior, intelligence and education gave him the respect of his comrades, and appealing to the prejudice against the "Yankees," which the disastrous results of the Mexican war had not tended to lessen in their minds, he soon assembled around him a powerful band of his countrymen, who daily increased, as he ran his career of almost magical success. Among the number was Manuel Garcia, more frequently known as "Three fingered Jack," from the fact of his having had one of his fingers shot off in a skirmish with an American party during the Mexican war. He was a man of unflinching bravery, but cruel and sanguinary. His form was large and rugged, and his countenance so fierce that few liked to look upon it. He was different from his more youthful leader, in possessing nothing of his generous, frank and cordial disposition, and in being utterly destitute of one merciful trait of humanity.

His delight was in murder for its own diabolical sake, and he gloated over the agonies of his unoffending victims. He would sacrifice policy, the safety and interests of the band for the mere gratification of this murderous propensity, and it required all Joaquin's firmness and determination to hold him in check. The history of this monster was well known before he joined Joaquin. He was known to be the same man, who, in 1846, surrounded with his party two Americans, young men by the names of Cowie and Fowler, as they were traveling on the road between Sonoma and Bodega, stripped them entirely naked, and, binding them each to a tree, slowly tortured them to death. He began by throwing knives at their bodies, as if he were practicing at a target; he then cut out their tongues, punched out their eyes with his knife, gashed their bodies in numerous places, and, finally flaying them alive, left them to die.

A thousand cruelties like these had he been guilty of, and long before Joaquin knew him he was a hardened, experienced and detestable monster. When it was necessary for the young chief to commit some peculiarly horrible and cold-blooded murder, some deed of hellish ghastliness at which his soul revolted, he deputed this man to do it; and well was it executed, with certainty and to the letter.

Another member was the boy, Reyes Feliz, whom I have before mentioned, as the brother of Rosita, and who was left by his fugitive sister a year or so before in the province of Sonora. The old father, the packer, was dead, and Reyes, having no ill-feeling whatever against Joaquin and his sister, had hastened with the remnant of his father's' property, to join them, and had arrived in California a few weeks after the affair of the mob at Murphy's Diggings. He was now a mere youth of sixteen years, but he had read the wild romantic lines of the chivalrous robbers of Spain and Mexico, until his enthusiastic spirit had become imbrued with the same sentiments which actuated them, and he could conceive of nothing grander than to throw himself back upon the, strictly natural rights of man and hurl defiance at society and its laws. There is many a villain nowadays, for the mere romance of the thing. Reyes Feliz was a devoted follower of his chief; like him, brave, impulsive, and generous.

A third member was Claudio, a man about thirty-five years of age, of a lean, but vigorous constitution, a dark complexion and possessing a somewhat savage but lively and expressive countenance. He was indisputably brave, but exceedingly cautious and cunning, springing upon his prey at an unexpected moment and executing his purposes with the greatest possible secrecy as well as precision. He was a deep calculator, a wise schemer, and could wear the appearance of an honest man with the same grace and ease that he would exhibit in throwing around his commanding figure the magnificent cloak in which he prided.

In disposition he was revengeful, tenacious in his memory of at wrong, sly and secret in his windings as a serpent, and, with less nobility than the rattlesnake, he gave no warning before he struck. Yet, as I have said before, he was brave, when occasion called for courage, and although ever ready to take an advantage, ho never flinched in the presence of danger. This extreme caution, united with, a strong will and courage to do, made him an exceedingly formidable man.

A fourth member was Joaquin Vaenzuela, named in a preceding page. His chief threw upon him much responsibility in the government of the band, and entrusted him with important expeditions requiring in their execution a great amount of skill and experience. Vaenzuela was a much older man than his leader, and had acted for many years in Mexico as a bandit under the famous guerilla chief, Padre Jurata.

Another distinguished member was Pedro Gonzales, less brave than many others, but a skillful spy and expert horse thief, and, as such, an invaluable adjunct to a company of mounted men who required a continual supply of fresh horses, as well as a thorough knowledge of the state of affairs around them.

There were many others belonging to this organization, whom it is not necessary to describe. It is sufficient to say they composed as formidable a force of outlaws as ever gladdened the eye of an acknowledged leader. Their number at this early period is not accurately known, but a fair estimate would not place it at a lower figure than fifty, with the advantage of a continual and steady increase, including a few renegade Americans, of desperate characters and fortunes.

Besides Joaquín Murieta, there were others of the banditti who were accompanied by their mistresses. The names of these devoted but fair and frail ones will be of frequent occurrence in the succeeding pages.

Such was the unsettled condition of things, so distant and isolated were the different mining regions, so lonely and uninhabited the sections through which the roads and trails were cut, and so numerous the friends and acquaintances of the bandits themselves, that these lawless men carried on their operations with almost absolute impunity. It was a rule with them to injure no man who ever extended them a favor, and whilst they plundered every one else, and spread devastation in every other quarter, they invariably left those ranches and houses unharmed, whose owners and inmates had afforded them shelter or assistance.

Many persons who were otherwise honestly inclined, bought the safety of their lives and property by remaining scrupulously silent in regard to Joaquin, and neutral in every attempt to do him an injury. Further than this, there were many large rancheros who were secretly connected with the banditti, and stood ready to harbor them in times of danger, and to furnish them with the best animals that fed on their extensive pastures. The names of several of these wealthy and highly respectable individuals are well known, and will transpire in the course of this history.

At the head of this most powerful combination of men, Joaquin ravaged the State in various quarters during the year 1851, without at that time being generally known as the leader; his subordinates, Claudio, Valenzuela and Pedro Gonzalez, being alternately mistaken for the chief. Except to a few persons, even his name was unknown; and many were personally acquainted with him, and frequently saw him in the different towns and villages, without having the remotest idea that he stood connected with the bloody events which were then filling the country with terror and dismay. He resided for weeks at a time in different localities, ostensibly engaged in gambling, or employed as a vaquero, a packer, or in some other apparently honest avocation, spending much of his time in the society of that sweetest of all companions, the woman that he loved.

While living in a secluded part of the town of San Jose, sometime in the summer of '51, he one night became violently engaged in a row at a fandango, was arrested for a breach of the peace, brought up before a magistrate and fined twelve dollars. He was in charge of Mr. Clark, the Deputy Sheriff of Santa Clara County, who had made himself particularly obnoxious to the banditti, by his rigorous scrutiny into their conduct, and his determined attempts to arrest some of their number. Joaquin had the complete advantage of him, inasmuch as the Deputy was totally ignorant of the true character of the man with whom he had to deal. With the utmost frankness in his manner, Joaquin requested him to walk down to his residence in the skirts of the town, where he would pay him the money.

They proceeded together, engaged in a pleasant conversation, until they reached the edge of a thicket, when the young bandit suddenly drew a knife and informed Clark that he had brought him there to kill him, at the same instant stabbing him to the heart before he could draw his revolver. Though many persons knew the author of this most cool and bloody deed, by sight, yet it was a long time before it was ascertained that the escaped murderer was no less a personage than the leader of the daring cut-throats who, were then infesting the country.

In the fall of the same year, Joaquin removed up in the more northern part of the State, and settled himself down with his mistress at the Sonorian Camp, a cluster of tents and cloth houses, situated about three miles from the city of Marysville, in Yuba County. It was not long before the entire country rung with the accounts of frequent, startling and diabolical murders.

Seven men were murdered within three or four days in a region of country not more than twelve miles in extent.

Shortly after the murders thus mentioned, two men who were traveling on the road that leads up Feather River, near to the Honcut Creek, which puts into that stream, discovered just ahead of them four Mexicans, one of whom was dragging at his saddle-bow, by a lariat, an American whom they lad just lassoed around the neck. The travelers did not think it prudent to interfere, and so hurried on to a place of safety, and reported what they had seen. Legal search being made upon this information, four other men were found murdered near the same place, bearing upon their throats the fatal mark of the lariat.

Close upon these outrages, reports came that several individuals had been killed and robbed at Bidwell's Bar, some ten or fifteen miles up the river. Consternation spread like fire; fear thrilled the hearts of hundreds, and all dreaded to travel the public roads.

Suspicion was directed to the "Sonorian Camp," it being occupied exclusively by Mexicans, many of whom had no ostensible employment, and yet rode fine horses, and spent money freely. This suspicion was confirmed by a partial confession obtained from a Mexican thief, who had fallen into the hands of the "Vigilance Committee" of Marysville, and had been run up with a rope several times to the limb of a tree, by order of that formidable body.

He confessed to the commission of no crime himself, but pointed to the Sonorian Camp as the retreat of certain parties who had been carrying on the system of robberies and murders complained of. Obtaining a description of the principal characters at the suspected camp, the Sheriff of Yuba County, R. B. Buchanan, accompanied by a man familiarly known as "Ike Bowen," proceeded on a moonlight night to examine the premises, and to consummate an arrest of one or more, by surprise. Hitching their horses a half mile distant, they advanced on foot to the dangerous' neighborhood. Coming suddenly upon a small tent a few hundred yards from the main camp, not having observed it in the obscurity of the bushes, they were barked at by a ferocious dog, who appeared' likely by his fierce outcries to arouse the whole encampment.

"It won't do," said Buchanan, "to be bothered with such a howling as this, and we must kill that dog. It strikes me that I can manage it. If we appear to be frightened, and beat a retreat, he will come directly up to take hold of one or the other of us; then we inust let him have a little cold steel."

Accordingly the two moved off hastily, and, true to the prediction of Buchanan, the animal rushed forward with frantic ferocity. Bowen, being a little behind, he sprang with one bound upon his back, got him down in an instant, and was giving him more than under the circumstances, was at all comfortable, when Buchanan, having the beast at a disadvantage, drew a bowie-knife, and plunging it into his heart laid him dead on the spot. This done they continued their advances, but by the stirring to and fro on the outskirts of the camp, they soon perceived that the dog had given a little too much warning. In a somewhat isolated corner near a piece of fencing they discovered standing by a fire near an open tent, a Mexican wrapped in his *serappe* who was peering out anxiously into the shadows, and who appeared to answer to a description of one of the Sonorian desperados, as given by the thief heretofore mentioned as having been in the hands of the Vigilance Committee.

"Let us get down on our hands and knees," said Buchanan, "or we may be discovered."

Crawling in this manner they reached the fence, and looking through they discovered that the Mexican was missing.

"The fellow has seen us," observed Buchanan, "and we must look sharp or he and his crowd will have the advantage."

He and Bowen then commenced crawling through the bars of the fence, and while in the act were startled by three distinct shots, which were soon again repeated. Extricating themselves as soon as possible from the fence, they rose to their feet, and discovered three Mexicans blazing away at them with revolvers from a point near a bush, behind which they had been hidden. Of course the Sheriff and his assistant were not long in returning the fire, and a very brisk engagement ensued. The Mexicans, apparently unhurt, retired, and Buchanan and Bowen were left to their own company. The former then found that he had been severely wounded, and after walking a few hundred yards from the scene of conflict fell to the earth, and was unable to rise.

The ball had struck him near the spine, and passing through his body, had come out in front near the navel. He had evidently received it while in a stooping posture at the fence. Leaving him as he lay, Bowen hastened to his horse and hurried to town for assistance, which shortly arrived, and Buchanan was taken back to Marysville and properly cared for. He lay a long time in a very dangerous situation, but eventually recovered, much to the gratification of the community, who admired the devotion and courage with which he had well-nigh sacrificed his life to the, discharge of duty. He was somewhat astonished to learn, a considerable period afterward, that he had received his wound in an actual personal encounter with the redoubtable Joaquín Murieta himself. He it was who had been standing before the fire in front of the tent, and had with his quick eye discovered the two hostile forms as they approached him through the patches of moonlight.

III

DEPARTURE OF THE ROBBERS FOR THE COAST RANGE—MOUNT SHASTA THE GREAT LANDMARK—THE ROBBERS AMONG THE INDIAN—THE TALL MISOURIAN A DEAD SHOT—BLEACHING SKELETONS AND PERFORATED SKULLS—REYES FELIZ AND THE FAITHLESS SPOUSE—OLD PETER AND HIS TWO DAUGHTERS—THE LASSOING OF AN ELK BY THE ELDEST DAUGHTER—SHE FALLS INTO THE HANDS OF THE ROBBERS—HER TIMELY ESCAPE

The bandits did not long remain in the vicinity of Marysville after this occurrence, but rode off into the coast range of mountains to the west of Mount Shasta, which rears its white shaft, at all seasons of the year, high above every other peak, and serves at a distance of two hundred miles to direct the course of the mountain traveler. Gazing at it from the Sacramento Valley, it rises in its garments of snow, like some mighty archangel, filling the heaven with his solemn presence.

In the rugged fastnesses of the wild range lying to the west of this huge mount, a range inhabited only by human savages and savage beasts, did the outlaws hide themselves for several long months, descending into the valleys at intervals, with no further purpose than to steal horses, of which they seemed determined to keep a good supply. They induced the Indians to aid them in this *laudable* purpose, and so efficiently did these simple people render their assistance, that the rancheros of that region loaded the very air with their curses of the "naked devils," who tormented them to such an intolerable degree.

On one occasion, during these depredations upon locomotive property, an exasperated party of Americans, who had been on the track of their stolen animals, came up with the Indian thieves, and managed to hem them in between a perpendicular wall of bluffs and a deep river, so that there was no escape for them but to swim the stream, which swept by in a mad and foaming torrent. They fired upon the Indians, who leaped into the water, many of them dyeing it with their blood, and a few successfully swimming across. In the midst of the firing a tall Mexican, mounted upon a fine horse, dashed down the banks, firing his revolver as he went, and plunged into the stream. His horse struck, out boldly with him for the opposite shore, and he had gained the middle of the current, a distance of a, hundred yards from his pursuers, before any effectual shot at him was made.

He was about to escape, and nothing would now avail but a dead aim and a steady nerve. The best marksman in the crowd, a lank Missourian, dismounted from his horse, drew his rifle to his shoulder while the others looked anxiously on, and taking along "bead," fired. The Mexican leaned forward a moment and the next instant floated from the saddle and sunk, while his fine charger breasted the waves and ascended the bank with a snorting nostril and dripping mane. No one was willing to risk the dangerous passage even to possess so noble an animal, and they returned with their recovered property to, their homes. This tall Mexican was a member of Joaquin's band, who had led the Indians in that very unsuccessful, thieving expedition.

In that desolate region, through which, at long intervals, only few straggling miners passed, on their lonesome prospecting tours, human skeletons were, found bleaching in the sun, some leaving no trace of the manner in which they perished, while others plainly showed by the perforated skull that the leaden ball had suddenly and secretly done its work. The ignorant Indians suffered for many a deed which had been perpetrated by civilized hands. It will be recollected by many persons who resided at Yreka aid on Scott's River, in the fall and winter of 1851, how many prospectors were lost in the mountains and never again heard from; how many were found dead, supposed to have been killed by the Indians, and yet bearing upon their bodies the marks of knives and bullets quite as frequently as arrows.

In one of the descents of the banditti into the valleys, they ventured into the plains which skirted Feather River, and on the edge of which is situated the, town of Hamilton. This was a long distance from the coast range, but the fall months of 1851 were clear and mild, and camping out was a mere pastime. Here the bandits were frequently scattered, two or three riding together, others remaining at the temporary camp, others again running off horses from Neil's Ranch, and others playing cards in the saloons at Hamilton.

Reyes Feliz was in the habit of galloping around unaccompanied, for being a good-looking fellow, he found himself welcome at various Mexican camps along the river, where certain smiling senoritas happened to be located. At one of these camps he met with the wife of a packer, then absent with a pack train in the mountains. She was a voluptuous beauty, and named Carmelita. Reyes Feliz was not long in discovering that she fancied him, and he made rapid advances in her affections—so much so, he one day persuaded her that he was a better husband than the packer, and she agreed with very little hesitation to link her fortunes with those of the gay and gallant cavalier who had won her to his embraces. The bandits at the camp were therefore greatly surprised to see him one evening cantering in with a blooming fair one behind him, whom he deposited in their midst, with a nonchalent air and the brief introduction—"There's my wife."

Residing in the vicinity of Hamilton was a hunter, who was known by the simple name of "Peter." He was half Wyandot and half French, and had two daughters, aged respectively eighteen and sixteen. Old Peter was probably the most honest man in all that section of country. Ever since the death of his wife—half French and half Wyandot like himself—which had happened in Iowa many years before the time of his introduction to the reader, he had followed the life of a trapper and, hunter, taking his two girls along with him. He had remained some years in the Rocky Mountains, and thence had ranged down by gradual removes, into California. He had horses, a heavy tent, plenty of clothing, and a purse generally well filled with money. This he earned solely by hunting, there being a good cash market for all the venison and bear meat which he could furnish.

Peter prided himself upon two things, his own honesty and the virtue of his daughters. They were very handsome girls, and although trained up in the wilderness, yet they had sufficiently trod the confines of civilization to know something of its refining effects. Besides their father was by no means a savage, having received the rudiments of a French education in his youth, and having mingled with the better class of the border citizens of the United States to an extent which enabled him to speak pretty good English, and to act very much like a white man. But the Indian instinct was strong, both in himself and his daughters, the elder of whom was a dead shot with the rifle and a splendid rider, after the fashion of Indian women, to wit: astraddle.

She had learned also to throw the lasso, and had more than once brought into camp wild elks, lassoed around the horns and towed at her saddle bow. Strange as this may seem, it is literally true, and there are many persons now living in California who remember the girl and her feats. The younger sister, although skilled in the handicraft of the woods, was not so daring, but was exceedingly useful to her father by her knack at cooking, washing and attending to the domestic affairs of the camp.

The father usually wore a buckskin suit, while the garb of the girls consisted of a calico or woolen skirt and bodice, a silk handkerchief carelessly tied under the chin, and upon their small and well shaped feet handsomely beaded moccasins.

A couple of the bandits were one morning galloping over the plain, in the direction of a band of loose horses, with a view of lassoing one or two of them, when a huge elk rapidly crossed the line of their progress. The animal was making the best speed he could, and well he might, for not more than fifty yards behind there came thundering after him a mounted figure, with disheveled hair and eager eyes and urgent pressings of the pursuing steed. It was the old hunter's daughter, lasso in hand, enjoying her favorite pastime of elk-chasing.

It may well be conjectured that the bandits were somewhat astonished at this unusual sight, for they had never seen or heard of this extraordinary maiden before. Neither the elk nor the girl paid any attention to them, but dashed on, pursued and pursuing. The robbers, exhilarated by the spectacle, put spurs to their horses and followed in the chase. Onward sped the wild hunters for a mile or more, till now she gains upon the panting beast, reaches within twenty or thirty feet of him, whirls the adjusted loop around and around her head to give it impetus, and lets loose the springing coil. Forth it flies on its lengthened mission, and the noose drops down over the branching horns. The well-trained mustang stops short in his tracks, the cord tightens at the saddle-bow, and the flying elk, suddenly jerked backward, falls heavily to the ground. With a shout of applause the robbers recognize the capture and rein their chargers to the spot.

Addressing the girl in Spanish, they found she spoke English, and so conversed with her moderately well in that language. The elk being somewhat refractory, they politely offered to help her home with it, and did so, driving it forward while she galloped on ahead. Arriving at her father's camp, it was courtesy to ask the strangers to alight and refresh themselves. They partook of the wholesome repast spread before them by the younger sister, and I had finished their last cup of coffee, when old Peter entered. He looked at his newfound guests with a degree of suspicion, and saluted them but coldly. He took no apparent interest in the rehearsal of his daughter's adventure, and, when the strangers arose to depart he did not ask them to call again.

One of them, however, the smooth spoken and graceful Claudio, did call the next day, and old Peter peremptorily ordered him away. There was something in the old man's look that even as brave a scoundrel as Claudio did not like unnecessarily to parley with, and thinking, "discretion the better part of valor," he left. Old Peter, it seems, knew instinctively that he was a rascal, and was not disposed to waste, any ceremonious courtesy upon him.

After the expiration of a few days, the young Diana concluded to ride over into to the woods that skirt Butter Creek, a clear, pebbly-bottomed stream that empties into the Feather River, some distance above Hamilton. She took her rifle with her—a small-bored, silver-mounted piece, with an elegant curly maple stock—thinking that she would bring in a number of the gray squirrels with which the grounds abounded, for the purpose of converting them into pot-pie. The sharp crack of her rifle was the death-knell of many an "adjidaumo," and soon, with a string of the bushy-tailed "varmints," at her saddle-bow, she grew weary of the sport, and reclined for a brief rest upon a plot of dry grass underneath an oak tree, leaving her docile pony to feed at his discretion in the neighborhood.

It was not long before she fell asleep. How long she had slumbered she could not say, but she was suddenly awakened by a strong pressure upon her wrists, and opening her eyes in a fuller consciousness, she found herself in the grasp of a powerful man. It was the late companion of Claudio, in the matter of the elk adventure and the subsequent repast at old Peter's camp. The villain had secured the girl's wrists with a piece of cord, and now held a knife at her throat, threatening to kill her instantly if she dared to scream out. Nevertheless she did scream, until a gag was thrust into her mouth by a second party whom she had not until then discovered, and who proved to be Claudio. The two were proceeding to drag the terrified girl into an adjacent thicket, rendered well nigh impervious by a mazy entanglement of wild pea vines, when a horseman dashed up, and cocking his revolver, commanded the rascals to desist.

The girl was surprised to see that they instantly obeyed. She was unbound, her rifle restored to her and her pony led to where she was standing. After she was mounted, and on the point of departing, her strange rescuer rode closely up to her and said:

"Young woman, you've heard of Joaquín Murieta. I'm the man. When you hear people abusing me, hereafter, perhaps you'll think I'm not quite so big a scoundrel as they say I am, after all. Now, hurry home, before some other danger overtakes you."

With a grateful heart, the maiden bade him adieu, and galloped off. When at a distance of about a hundred yards, the group still gazing at her, she suddenly halted, and turned around as if to come back, but stood still, facing them. While they were wondering what on earth she could be at, they soon perceived that she was deliberately leveling her rifle to draw a "bead" on some one of the party. Claudio instinctively wheeled from the front of the tree, where he was standing, with a sudden effort to slide behind it, when the rifle cracked, and the bark flew from the exact spot at which he would have been struck to the heart if he had remained a moment longer. With a sharp feminine whoop and a gay laugh of defiance, the spirited damsel put wings to her horse's feet and was soon out of sight.

Old Peter, I have already said, was an honest man, but, much as he hated villains, he was never, heard, so long as he remained in the country, to speak a harsh word of the robber Joaquin.

IV

Trip of the Bandits to Sonora—They Take Up Headquarters at the Arroyo Cantoova—Joaquin's Felicity Under the Evergreen Oaks—He Divides His Company into Three Bands, Under Claudio, Valenzuela and Three-Fingered Jack, Leaving Himself Only a Few Attendants—The Women Dressed in Male Clothes—Joaquin a Visitor in the Towns, Unrecognized—His Daring Feat at Mokelumne Hill—Return of Ruddle—Comic Adventure Among the Digger Indians

As soon as the spring opened in 1852, Joaquin and his party descended from the mountains, and by forced marches in the night, drove some two or three hundred horses which they had collected at their winter rendezvous, down through the southern portion of the State, into the province of Sonora. Returning in a few weeks, they took up their headquarters at the Arroyo Cantoova, a fine tract of rich pasturage containing seven or eight thousand acres, beautifully watered, and fenced in by a circular wall of mountains, through which an entrance was afforded by a narrow gate or pass, at which a very formidable force could be stayed in their progress by a small body of men.

This rich and fertile basin lies halfway between the Tejon and the Pacheco Pass, to the east of the Coast Range, and to the west of the great Tulare Lake, thoroughly embosomed in its rugged boundaries, and the more valuable as a retreat, that it was distant at least one hundred and fifty miles from any human habitation. From the surrounding eminences an approaching enemy could be seen for a long way off. This region was in one respect in particular, adapted to the purpose for which it was chosen, and that is, it abounded in game of every kind: elk, antelope, deer, grizzly bears, quails, grouse, and every species of smaller animals, most desirable for food.

Here Joaquin selected a clump of evergreen oaks for his residence, and many a pleasant day found him and his still blooming companion, roofed by the rich foliage of the trees, and reclining upon a more luxurious carpet than ever blossomed with its imitative flowers, beneath the satin-slippered feet of the fairest daughters of San Francisco. The brow of his sweet and faithful friend would sometimes grow sad, as she recurred to the happy and peaceful lives which they had once lived, but with a woman's true nature, she loved him in spite of all his crimes, and her soul was again lighted up as she gazed into those dark and glorious eyes which had never quailed before mortal man, and lost their fierceness only when they looked on *her*.

Besides, in her tender heart she made for him many allowances; she saw many strong palliations of his conduct in the treatment which he had received; she knew the secret history of his soul, his sufferings, and his struggles with an evil fate, and the long agony which rent up by the roots the original honesty of his high born nature. More than this, he had told her that he would soon finish his dangerous career, when, having completed his revenge, and having accumulated an equivalent for the fortune of which he had been robbed by the Americans, he would retire into a peaceful portion of the State of Sonora, build him a pleasant home and live alone for love and her.

She believed him, for he spoke a truly of his intentions, and wonder not, ye denizens of cities she was happy, even in the wilderness. It mattered not how the world regarded him, to her he was is all that was noble, generous and beautiful.

After spending a few weeks at the rendezvous, Joaquin divided his party, then consisting of about seventy men, in to different bands, headed by Claudio, Three-Fingered Jack, and Valenzuela, and dispatched them, to various quarters, with orders to devote themselves chiefly to stealing horses and mules, as he had a purpose to effect which required at least fifteen hundred or two thousand animals. He himself, started on a separate course, accompanied by Reyes Feliz, Pedro Gonzalez, and Juan. Three females, who were dressed in male attire and well-armed, were also in company; that is to say, Joaquin's mistress, and those of Reyes Feliz and Pedro Gonzalez. All the party were well mounted, and rode, no one knew whither, except Joaquin himself. Arriving at Mokelumne Hill, in Calaveras County, they took up quarters with some of their Mexican acquaintances in that place, and, passing through the streets, or visiting the saloons, were looked upon as nothing more than peaceable Mexicans, residing in the town.

This was in the month of April. While here, the women appeared in their proper attire, and were admired for their exceedingly, modest and quiet deportment. The men issued forth at night upon no praise-worthy missions, and, mounted upon their magnificent chargers, scoured an extent of many miles ere they returned stealthily back to their hiding place, and the arms of their languishing loves. Joaquin bore the appearance and character of an elegant and successful gambler, being amply provided with means from his night excursions.

In the meantime his men were, in different directions, prosecuting with ardor the business upon which they had been sent, and there was a universal cry throughout the lower country, that horse thieves were very neatly impoverishing the ranchos. Joaquin gathered a pretty good knowledge of what his followers were about from the newspapers, which made a very free use of his own name, in the accounts of these transactions, and handled his character in no measured terms. In the various outbreaks in which he had been personally engaged; he had worn different disguises, and was actually disguised the most when he showed his real features. No man who had met him on the highway would be apt to recognize him in the cities.

He frequently stood very unconcernedly in a crowd, and listened to long and earnest conversations in relation to himself; and laughed, in his sleeve at the many conjectures which were made as to his whereabouts and intentions.

After remaining as long as he desired at Mokelumne Hill; about the first of May he prepared to take his departure, which he resolved to do at the hour of midnight. His horses were saddled, the women dressed in their male clothes, and everything ready, when Joaquin sauntered out into the streets, according to his custom, and visited the various drinking and gambling saloons, with which every California town and village abound. While sitting at a monte table, at which he carelessly put down a dollar or two to while away the time, his attention was suddenly arrested by the distinct pronunciation of his name just opposite to where he sat.

Looking up, he observed three or four Americans engaged in loud and earnest conversation in relation to himself, in which one of them, a tall fellow, armed with a revolver, re-marked that he "would just like once in his life to come across Joaquin, and that he would kill him as quick as he would a snake." The daring bandit, upon hearing this speech, jumped upon the monte table in view of the whole house, and drawing his six-shooter, shouted out:

"I am Joaquin! If there is any shooting to do I am in!"

So sudden and startling was this movement that every one quailed before him, and in the midst of the consternation and confusion which reigned, he gathered his cloak about him and walked out unharmed.

After this bold avowal of himself, it was necessary for him to make his stay quite short in that vicinity. Mounting his horse therefore with expedition, he dashed off with his party at his heels, sending back a whoop of defiance, which rung out thrillingly in the night air. The extreme chagrin of the citizens, can be imagined when they found; for the first time, that they had unwittingly tolerated in their very midst the man whom, above all others, they would have wished to secure.

Returning to his rendezvous at Arroyo Cantoova, he found that his marauding bands had gathered some two or three hundred head of horses, and were patiently waiting his further orders. He detached a portion of them to take the animals into Sonora for safe keeping, and made remittances of money at the same time to a secret partner of his in that State.

Towards the last of May, becoming again restless, and tired of an inactive life; he started forth upon the highroads, attended as before, when on his visit to Mokelumne-Hill, simply by Reyes Feliz, Pedro Gonzalez, Juan and the three bright-eyed girls, who, mounted on very elegant chargers, appeared as charming a trio of handsome cavaliers as ever delighted the visions of romantic damsels. Meeting with no one for a week or two but impoverished Frenchmen, and dilapidated Germans, in search of "diggins," and having sent very nearly all his money to Sonora, Joaquin's purse was getting rather low, and he resolved to attack the first man or men he might meet, who appeared to be supplied. He was this time on the road to San Luis Gonzagos, to which place a young American, named Albert Ruddle, was at the time driving a wagon loaded with groceries.

Overtaking this young man on an open plain, Joaquin, leaving his party behind, rode up to him where he sat upon one of his wheel horses, and politely bidding him "good morning," requested of him the loan of what small change he might have about him, remarking at the same moment:

"It is true I am a robber, but, as sure as I live, I merely wish to *borrow* this money, and I will as certainly pay it back to you as my name is Joaquin. It is not often that I am without funds, but such is my situation at present."

Ruddle, without replying, made a sudden motion to draw his pistol, upon which Joaquin exclaimed:

"Come, don't be foolish—I have no wish to kill you, and let us have no fight."

Ruddle made another effort to get his pistol, which, from excitement, or perhaps from its hanging in the holster, he could not instantly draw, when the bandit, with a muttered oath, slashed him across the neck with his bowie knife and dashed him from the saddle. Searching his pockets, he found about three hundred dollars. His party coming up, he rode on, leaving the murdered map where he lay, and his wagon and team standing by the road. Joaquin's conscience smote him for this deed, and he regretted the necessity of killing so honest and hard working a man as Ruddle seemed to be.*

It happened that just at this period, Capt. Harry Love, whose own history is one of equal romance with that of Joaquin, but marked only with events which redound to his honor, was at the head of a small party, gotten up on his own responsibility, in search of this outrageous bandit. Love had served as an express rider in the Mexican war, and had borne despatches from one military post to another, over the most dangerous tracts of Mexico. He had traveled alone for hundreds of miles over mountains and deserts, while beset with a no less danger than the dreaded "guerillas," who hung o upon the skirts of the American army, laid in wait at mountain passes and watering places, and made it their business to murder every unfortunate straggler that fell into their hands. Riding fleet horses, and expert in the use of the his lasso, it required a well mounted horseman to escape them on the open plains, and many a hard race with them has the Captain had to save his neck and the valuable papers in his charge. He had been, moreover, from his early youth, a hardy pioneer, experienced in all the dangers and hardships of a border life.

Having these antecedents in his favor and possessing the utmost coolness in danger, he was a man well fitted to contend with a person like Joaquin, than whom the lightning was not quicker and surer in the execution of a deadly errand. Love was on the direct trail of Joaquin, when Ruddle was murdered. With the utmost speed consistent with the caution necessary to a surprise of the bandit, he pursued him by his murders and robberies, which left a bloody trail behind him, to the rancho of San Luis Gonzagos, which is now well known to have been a place which regularly harbored the banditti. Arriving at that place at night, he ascertained by certain spies whom he had employed, that the

---

* This circumstance was related to the writer by a man named Brown, who was intimate with Joaquin, and whom the robber talked freely.

party of whom he was in search, were staying in a canvas house on the edge of the rancho.

Proceeding cautiously to this house with his men, the Captain had just reached the door, when the alarm was given by a woman in a neighboring tent, and in an instant Joaquin, Gonzalez, Reyes Feliz and Juan had cut their way through the back part of the canvas and escaped into the darkness. On entering, no one was to be seen but women, three of whom, then dressed in their proper garments, were the bandits' mistresses, of which fact, however, Love was ignorant. Leaving the women to shift for themselves, the fugitives went to their horses, which were hitched in an adjacent thicket, mounted them, and rode directly over to Oris Timbers, a distance of eight miles, where they immediately stole twenty head of horses, and drove them off into the neighboring mountains.

They remained concealed all the next day, but at night came back (a movement wholly unanticipated by Love) to the cloth house where they had left their women, who quickly doffed their female attire, and rode off With their companions in the hills, from which they had just come. Driving the stolen horses before them, the parties started in high glee across the Tulare Plains, for Los Angeles. Love followed them no further, having business which recalled him. The owner of the Oris Timbers Rancho, however, attended by a few Americans, fell upon their trail, indicated by the Captain, and pursued them without much difficulty into the country of the Tejon Indians.

Not coming up with them, and perhaps not very anxious to do so, the owner of the horses proceeded with his attendants to the seat of government of the Tejon Root Digger Nation, in order to see the old chief, Sapatarra, and if possible to make an arrangement with him by which to recover his property. They soon reached the capital, which consisted of twenty or thirty very picturesque-looking bark huts, scattered along the side of a hill, in front of the largest of which they found old Sapatarra, seated upon his haunches in all the grandeur of "naked majesty," enjoying a very luxurious repast of roasted acorns and tried angle-worms. His swarthy subjects were scattered in various directions around him, engaged for the most part in the very arduous task of doing nothing.

The little smoky-looking children were sporting, like a black species of water fowl, in the creek which ran a short distance below, while the women were pounding with stone pestles in stone mortars, industriously preparing their acorn bread. The delicacies of the chiefs table were soon: spread before his guests, which, though, tempting, they respectfully declined, and entered immediately upon their business. Sapatarra was informed that a party of Mexican horse thieves had sought shelter in his boundaries; that they were only a few in number, and they had in their possession twenty splendid horses, one half of which should belong to the chief if he recovered the whole number. This arrangement was speedily effected, and the high contracting parties separated with great satisfaction, and mutual assurances of their distinguished regard.

Sapatarra held a council of state, which resulted in sending spies over his dominions to discover traces of the marauding band. Information was returned in a day or two, that seven Mexicanos, superbly dressed, and covered with splendid jewelry, and having a large number of fine horses, were camped on a little stream about fifteen miles from the capital. The cupidity of the old chief and his right-hand men was raised to the highest pitch, and they resolved to manage the matter in hand with great skill and caution; which last, by the way, is a quality that particularly distinguishes the California Indians, amounting to so extreme a degree that it might safely be called cowardice. Joaquin and party, having ascertained that they were no longer pursued by the Oris Timber Ranchero, and feeling perfectly secure amongst so harmless a people as the Tejons, disencumbered themselves of their weapons and resolved to spend a few days in careless repose and genuine rural enjoyment.

Juan was one evening lying in the grass watching the horses as they fed around him, while Gonzalez, Feliz and Murieta were each of them separately seated under a live-oak tree, enjoying a private *tete a tete* with their beloved and loving partners. The evening shades were softly stealing around them, and all nature seemed to lull their unquiet spirits to security and repose. Just at this moment a few dark figures might have been seen, but unfortunately were not, creeping cat-like in the direction of the unsuspecting Juan, and the unconscious Murieta, Goonzalez and the others. It was well managed.

By a sudden and concerted movement the whole party were seized, overpowered, and securely bound before they were aware of what was going on. The Indians were in ecstasies at this almost unhoped for success, for had the least resistance been made, a single pistol cocked, or a knife drawn, they would have left the ground on the wings of the wind—so largely developed is the bump of caution on the head of a

California Indian! But cunning is equally developed, and serves their purposes quite as well sometimes as downright courage. As soon as this feat was accomplished, the woods became alive with forms, faces and voices.

A triumphal march was made with the captives to the capital. They were stripped entirely naked, and their rich clothing covered the weather-beaten backs and scaly legs of the Tejons; but great was the astonishment of the natives, when they discovered the sex of the three youthful cavaliers, who were kindly permitted, in pity for their modesty, to wear some of the old cast-off shifts that lay around in the dirt among the huts. The women were robbed of their jewelry to the amount of three thousand dollars, and the men of seven thousand dollars in gold dust, besides their riding animals and stolen horses. They were left also without a solitary weapon. Never were men so humiliated. The poor, miserable, cowardly Tejons had achieved a greater triumph over them than all the Americans put together.

Joaquin looked grim for a while, but finally burst into a loud laugh at his ridiculous position, and he ever afterwards endured his captivity with a quiet smile.

The "most potent, grave and reverend seignor," Sapatarra, immediately despatched one half of the stolen horses to the Otis Timbers while he retained the other, according to agreement. He kept his "prisoners of war" in custody for a week or two, debating in his mind, whether to make targets of them the for his young men to practice archery upon, or to hang, burn or drown them. He finally sent word to "the great Capitan," the County Judge of Los Angeles, that he had a party of Mexicans in custody, and wanted his advice as what to do with them. The Judge, supposing that the capture was the result of a little feud between some "greasers" and the Tejons, advised him to release them.

Accordingly one fine morning, the prisoners under the supervision of Sapatarra, surrounded by his guard, who were armed with the revolvers and knives which they had taken from the bandits, were led forth from the village with such solemnity that they imagined that they were going to none other than a place of execution. Arrived at a group of live-oaks, they were bound, naked, the women included, each to a tree.

Sapatarra, dressed for the occasion with a broad-brimmed hat and a bob-tailed red flannel shirt, which gave his ancient and venerable legs a most unique appearance, made a long speech which was a mixture of Digger and Spanish, on the merits of the transaction that was about to occur, enlarging upon the enormity of the crime which had been committed, (although it looked very much like self-condemnation in him to denounce stealing, inasmuch as the old fellow had himself stolen many a horse and eaten him besides!) and went off into extreme glorification over the magnanimity which would allow such great rascals to escape with their lives.

He then gave orders to have them whipped, and seven large, stout fellows stepped forth, shed their newly acquired shirts for a freer play of limb, and, with a bunch of willow rods, each to his place, gave the unfortunate party a very decent and thorough flogging.

Sapatarra then declared the ends of justice satisfied, and dismissed the prisoners from custody.

Poor fellows! They went forth into the wilderness as naked as on the day they were born, and stricken with a blanker poverty than the veriest beggar upon the streets of London or of New York. The biters were bit, the robbers were robbed, and loud and deep were the curses which Feliz, Juan and Gonzalez pronounced upon Sapatarra and the whole Tejon nation. But Joaquin rubbed his snarting back and laughed prodigiously, declaring upon his honor as a man that not a hair of old Sapatarra's head should be harmed at any time in the future.

V

Movements of the Naked Party—Reyes Feliz Meets with a Grizzly Bear—Self-Sacrificing Female Devotion—Sudden Relief From Distress—The Robber Chief Armed Again—Convenient Harboring Places at the Ranches of Wealthy Mexicans—Death of Pedro Gonzalez—Joaquin's Cold Assassination of the Deputy Sheriff of Santa Barbara County—Murder of Gen. Bean by Three-Fingered Jack and Joaquin—Meeting Between Joaquin and Joe Lake—Death of the Latter

The night succeeding their dismissal by old Sapatarra, they slept in the woods, naked as they were, without a stitch of covering; but fortunately it was near the summer, and the air possessed a merely pleasant coolness. The next day, in passing through an arroya, Reyes Feliz who was behind, was attacked by a grizzly bear, and after being horribly mangled in the jaws of the ferocious beast, only escaped instant destruction by feigning death. The bear having turned him over two or three times with his nose, slowly paced off into the thicket. The cries of Feliz for help meantime brought back his companions, who could, however, do him no good, not even so much as to staunch his wounds, having, as the reader is aware, not a stitch to their backs nor a rag in possession.

The bleeding youth with stoical endurance, begged his companions to leave him to his fate, as he believed that he must certainly die, and their attendance could be of no benefit to him. Seeing the necessity of moving on to some place where they could obtain food and clothing, they removed him to a shady place among some rocks near to a stream of water and left him to die—all but his sorrowing mistress, who resolved to remain: with him whatever might befall. They turned to look as they departed, and the last they saw was the faithful girl, with the lover's head upon her lap, pouring her tears upon him like a healing balm from her heart. Give me not a sneer thou rigid righteous! For the love of woman is beautiful at all times, whether she smiles under gilded canopies, in her satin garments, or weeps over a world-hated criminal, alone and naked in a desert.

After a day or two's travel, Joaquin and party arrived, nearly worn out, in the vicinity of the San Francisco Rancho at the Tejon Pass, where they met with Mountain Jim, an American desperado and co-operator with Joaquin's band, who had been out upon his "own hook," robbing and stealing for a few weeks then past. He was astounded at the spectacle which they presented, and begged Joaquin to allow him the privilege of laughing one good hearty laugh, before he listened to any explanation of the mystery. The privilege was readily granted, and the jolly bandit went through the performance with great zest and unction, making the woods echo and re-echo with his most refreshing peals of merriment. The women hid themselves in the brush, and were like mother Eve of the hotels making no concealment of his purpose to take him, dead or alive.

The next night after this discovery, a great excitement was raised in the street, and a crowd rushed up to see an apparently very hard fist fight between two Indians in front of the hotel at which Wilson was stopping. He, in common with others, stepped out to witness it, and was looking on with much interest, when a dashing young fellow rode up by his side on a fine horse, and stooping over his saddle bow, hissed in his ear, "I am Joaquin."

The astounded hearer started at the sentence, and had scarcely looked around before a pistol ball penetrated his skull, and he fell dead to the earth.

With his accustomed whoop, the daring murderer put spurs to his animal and galloped off. The fight between the Indians was a sham affair got up by Three-Fingered Jack to effect the very purpose which was consummated.

As the immediate consequence of this act, Los Angeles became too hot a place for the robbers to stay in; for the whole community was aroused and thirsting for vengeance. Accordingly Joaquin held a hasty conference with his followers, which resulted in sending Valenzuela and band, accompanied by Mountain Jim, into San Diego County, with directions to steal horses and convey them to Arroyo Cantoova, while Three-Fingered Jack with his band should accompany his chief wherever he might choose to go. Choosing to return once more to San Gabriel, they started in that direction, and met with no incident or individual on the road until they came to a dark hollow, walled on each side with precipitous rocks, through which a noisy stream was leaping and glancing in the moonlight; at this place two helpless Chinaman were encamped by the foot of a sycamore tree, and it being near eleven o'clock at night, were sleeping off their fatigue and the effects of their luxurious pipes of opium.

Their pick and prospecting pans showed them to be miners, who were most probably supplied with a due amount of cash, as Chinamen generally are Joaquin was for riding on, but Three-Fingered Jack could not resist the temptation of at least giving their pockets an examination. He therefore dismounted and walked up to the unconscious Celestials, who were snoring very loudly in their blankets; and shook them. They awoke, and seeing a horrible looking devil standing over, and glaring upon them, raised a hideous shriek, and rising, fell upon their knees before him, with the most lugubrious supplications, in a by no means euphonious tongue. Jack told them to "dry up," but they continued pleading for mercy, when he knocked one of them down with his revolver, and cocking it presented it at the head of the other, who closed his eyes in an agony of despair. In a voice of thunder he told the terrified Chinaman to "shell out," or he would blow a hole through him in a minute.

Readily convinced of the truth of this remark, the poor fellow nervously jerked out his purse and handed it to the robber, and searching the pocket of his companion, who lay stunned by his side, took out his also and presented it with a shudder. The amount was small—not more than twenty or thirty dollars—which so enraged the sanguinary monster that he drew his knife and cut both of their throats, before Joaquin could possibly interfere to prevent it. The young chief, who always regretted unnecessary cruelty, but knew full well that he could not dispense with so brave a man as Garcia, said nothing to him, but only groaned and rode on. The party reached San Gabriel without' further incident, and there related this last adventure.

General Bean, a man of influence and wealth, had, during Joaquin's absence, been giving serious trouble to' Claudio and band, who had been compelled to, lie out in the woods to avoid him. Joaquin himself thought it prudent to keep out of his way, and he lay concealed with Claudio for the space of six weeks, having with him Three-Fingered Jack and band. Portions of the banditti had regularly watched every opportunity to kill Gen. Bean, but, up to this time, had signally failed in every attempt. One evening, however, a spy having seen him start from his store at San Gabriel on horseback in the direction of his home, a few miles off, Three-Fingered Jack and Joaquin started by themselves to head around him and waylay him on the road.

They had scarcely taken their positions behind some rocks before Bean rode up. Joaquin sprung out in front of him and seizing the bridle, which had a Spanish bit, jerked his horse back upon his haunches, and just at that moment Three-Fingered Jack dragged him from the saddle and threw him upon the ground. At the moment that Jack laid hold of him he was in the act of firing at Joaquin, but being pulled back so suddenly, his pistol flew up many feet above the proper level and was discharged into the empty air. Bean being a powerful man, rose to his feet with Three-Fingered Jack upon him, and, drawing his knife, endeavored to use it, but his equally powerful antagonist seized his wrist with his left hand, and drawing in his turn a glittering bowie knife, sheathed it three times in his breast, then withdrawing the bloody blade he rudely shoved him back, and the brave but unfortunate man fell dead at his feet. The ignoble wretch, not satisfied with the successful termination of the combat, displayed his brutal disposition by kicking the dead body in the face, and discharging two loads from his revolver into the lifeless head.

Thus perished General Bean, a generous, noble hearted and brave man. Had he been less brave, he might have exercised more caution and preserved his life; but he was a man who never knew fear.

After this outrage, which though dark enough, was yet only an act of self-preservation on the part of Joaquin he collected his whole party in the neighborhood of the Mission, and started again on his ever restless course. He bent his way northward into Calaveras County, robbing a few pedding Jews, two or three Frenchmen and a Chinaman, as he went along, and giving an American express agent a fearful race for his life on an open plain, for, five or six miles, in which he distinctly heard no less than twenty bullets whiz by his head, and arrived in the vicinity of the town of Jackson in the latter part of the month of August.

Riding along one evening in advance of his men, as was frequently his custom, he met an old acquaintance who had been an esteemed friend in his more honest and happy days, a young man whose name was Joe Lake. Joaquin was delighted to see him, and rode up to him and embraced him, as they both sat on their horses, with that generous warmth of feeling which made an otherwise unmeaning custom of the Mexicans beautiful.

"Joe," said he, as he brushed a tear from his eyes, "I am not the man that I was; I am a deep-dyed scoundrel, but so help me God! I was driven to it by oppression and wrong. I hate my enemies; who are almost all the Americans, but I love *you* for the sake of old times. I don't ask you, Joe, to love or respect me, for an honest man like you cannot, but I do ask you not to betray me. I am unknown in this vicinity, and no one will suspect my presence, if you do not tell that you have seen me. My former good friend, I would rather do anything in the world than kill you, but if you betray me I will certainly do it."

Lake assured him that there was no danger, and the two parted, for the wide gulf of dishonor yawned between them, and they could never again be united. Lake rode over to the little town of Hornitas, and feeling it to be his duty to warn the citizens that so dangerous a man was in their midst, told a few Americans quite privately that he had seen the bloody cut-throat Murieta.

A Mexican was standing by wrapped in his *serape*, who bent his head on his bosom and smiled. About sundown of the next day, a solitary horseman, whose head was covered with a profusion of *red hair*, rode up very leisurely to the front of a trading post, at which Lake and some other gentlemen were standing, politely raised his hat, and addressed an inquiry to Lake, which caused him to step forward from the crowd the better to converse.

"Is your name Lake?" said the red haired stranger.

"The same," was the reply.

"Well sir, I am Joaquin! You have *lied* to me."

Lake being unarmed, exclaimed, "Gentlemen, protect me," and sprang back towards the crowd.

Several persons drew their revolvers, but not before the quick hand of Joaquin had presented his and pulled the trigger. The aim was fatal, and Lake fell in the agonies of death. The murderer wheeled his horse in an instant, and by a sudden bound, passed the aim of the revolvers which were discharged at him. In another instant he was seen on the summit of a hill, surrounded by no less than fifty well-mounted men, with whom he slowly rode off.

Such was the magical luck which pursued this man, following him like an invisible guardian fiend, in every hour of his peril, and enabling him to successfully perform deeds which would turn any other man's blood cold. So perfect was the organization which he had established that that apparently harmless Mexican who was standing near while Lake betrayed Joaquin, and who lived unsuspected in that very town, was none other than a paid member of his band, who acted as a spy.

VI

Joaquin Seeks a Respite From Annoyances—He Travels into Hitherto Unexplored Regions—Finds the Mysterious Lake of Mono—Strange Sights and Wonders—A Marvelous Mountain, Since Seen By Others—Description of its Singular Aspect and Phenomena—Discovery of Sculptured Antiquities and Ancient Burial Places—Singular Domicile For a Toad—A Weird Realm

Such daring feats as the one last recorded, and such equally daring and bloody ones as those which immediately preceded it, caused the organization of so many formidable companies of armed men, in the different counties through which the robber chief had more recently passed, sworn to capture him, that he became somewhat tired of the exercise of so much vigilance as the circumstances required of him, and concluded to spend the remaining portion of the dry season in some spot in the mountains which should be absolutely free from intrusion. Accordingly, not caring whither he went, so that he reached a secluded place, he struck out, with his whole band, in an easterly direction, taking along with the company, at the request of certain members whom he wished to please, a number of free and easy senoritas from the town of Jackson. Beside these were his own beautiful partner, and the wife of the late Gonzalez, who had already consoled her widowhood with an ugly, brutish member of the band named Guerra. Carmelita remained at San Gabriel with Reyes Feliz, who was still languid and feeble by his wounds from the grizzly bear.

The party, after two days' riding found themselves at the summit of the Sierra. Nevada, whence they descended towards the great Utah Basin. Passing down a succession of slopes, wooded with pine and juniper, they suddenly entered into an evidently new and unexplored region, alternating in sandy plains covered with sage bushes and rocky, intervening hills, dotted with stinted cedar, and enlivened with small valleys, which were watered by bright and sparkling streams.

Following one of these they discovered that it emptied—as they could trace it for a long distance by its willowy margin, and gradual descent—into a vast lake. As they approached this sheet of water they felt an increasing warmth in the atmosphere, and pretty soon a hot wind from the direction of the lake. Suddenly, as if to belie the heat, there came down upon them what appeared a terrific snow storm, but they soon discovered that there was no moisture in the flakes, and that they did not melt either upon themselves or their horses, but left both with a ghastly whiteness which it was difficult to shake off. When they told of this event afterward they did not even then know what to make of it, but the writer has since learned that a similar phenomenon has occurred at Washoe and other points on the rim of the Utah Basin, and is simply a shower of alkali dust caught up by the whirlwinds in the adjacent deserts, and descending, when their force is spent.

Astonished beyond measure at this circumstance, so much so that even Three-Fingered Jack crossed himself, and prayed to the Virgin Mary, while the hitherto gay femininies offered at the shrine of the same Virgin vows of eternal chastity. They rode on, and the sham snow storm being past they reined up on the margin of the expanse of water to which they had been for so many miles tending. Here, although prepared for almost anything that might happen, by what they had recently passed through, they were struck with new wonders. And well they might be, for they were on the shore of an inland sea, as mysterious as might have been.

— the dim lake of Auber,
In the ghoul-haunted woodland of Wier."

They stood by what is now known as Lake Mono, the name which was given it by the Indians who inhabit that region.

This lake, now included in the newly organized county of Mono, marked at that time the probable junction of the, somewhat vaguely defined boundary, lines of Calaveras, Mariposa and Fresno counties. It is twenty-seven miles long, and sixteen broad, curving somewhat in the shape of a crescent with a large island in the middle, five miles in length and whitened on the edges with peculiar incrustations. A white vapor, like incense from an altar, continually rises from this island, caused by the presence of the hot springs which it contains; and the subterranean heat is such that although a night's lodging on the island, is tolerable, it is not altogether comfortable. Nevertheless there are also springs of fresh water in the island, and some salt. Near by is a smaller island, lying dim and dingy by the side of the other.

Although the waters of the lake are clear, they have a Lethe-like and drowsy appearance, and within their slumbering depths no living thing is found, with the single exception of an insect, which is peculiar to the lake, and which has been discovered nowhere else in the world. This nondescript is shaped somewhat like a snail, has something like rudimental wings, is about three-quarters of an inch long, and of a brownish color.

They skim in swarms over the surface, or crawl upon the bottom, and in mild weather myriads are heaped upon the shore, and stretched out at times in living masses, as many as three feet deep. They constitute food for the miserable Root Diggers who haunt those parts, and also glut the innumerable gulls that roost on the island and occasional rocks which break the mirror of the water. The birds named form the only life above the surface, unless we except a few desolate and lonesome looking cranes, whose melancholy silence well harmonizes with the scene. But, in the winter season, uncounted multitudes of ducks and geese flock thither and make havoc upon their only spoil, the amphibious insect.

The slow, but steady flow of the waters is from the circumference to the centre, which is of unfathomable depth, indicating a subterranean gulf uinderneath. A perceptible difference in the temperature of the water in different parts would seem to signify that there might be hot jets shooting up from the bottom in the more shallow places. Although numerous streams of fresh water continually disembogue in the lake, its contents are so strongly impregnated with alkaline matter as to be unfit for use. This curious lake is about eight thousand feet above the level of the sea.

Seeing a curling smoke on a piece of table land belted with pines and cedars about a mile distant, Joaquin and party galloped in that direction. Arriving at the spot they discovered an Indian village composed of a few scattered brush houses, from which a set of scraggy figures, big and little, male and female, were scampering in great consternation. Joaquin told Juan to catch one of them and bring him back. Juan dismounted and started to execute the job. After a hard race he succeeded, and returned with a terrified native, a weather beaten veteran, whom he jerked along somewhat unceremoniously by the top of his head, and wheeled into the circle of the admiring spectators, for the purpose of having him give an account of himself.

It was difficult to persuade the poor fellow that he was not to suffer instant death. But his mind being relieved, he proceeded to make himself as intelligible as the nature of the case would admit of. Hearing him call the lake, to which they pointed, "Mono," which is a word in the Spanish signifying monkey, Joaquin addressed him in Spanish, but found that he knew nothing of the language. The fact is, "Mono" is an Indian term, its similarity to a Spanish word being merely accidental, as in the case of the Chinese "Sam Lee," or "Ah Come," which are comically suggestive to the speaker of English. The proper definition of the Indian "Mono" is not settled; some saying that it signifies Stranger, and others Dead Sea.

Releasing the poor Digger, they left him to explain matters and things to the balance of his tribe as he best could, and proceeded to a little valley, where there was some bunch grass, and encamped for the night. Having packed with them a supply of provisions which were not yet exhausted, and having feminine hands to prepare their meal, the time passed off pleasantly enough, and jest and song went round.

The curiosity of the bandits being satisfied after a few day's exploration of this region, and thinking they might see as new and as strange sights further on, they broke up camp and journeyed along the eastern slopes of the Sierra Nevada, southward. They found many beautiful resting places, where they tarried for a day or two, according as the fancy seized them. Still in search of incident and novelty, they kept their course southward—the character of the country varying between that of undulating plains, covered with sage brush, and rugged hills and mountain spurs, together with abyssmal vales, through which precipitous streams thundered—until they arrived at the eastern verge of Tulare county.

Here they again came into a region of striking desolation, and were destined to meet with new and undreamed of marvels. It was a rough tract of broken mountains, seeming to be separate and apart from the Sierra Nevada Range, whose sublime peaks rose on the right, crowned with snow, and its entire face was blackened and, crisped from the effects of volcanic action. It was a region treeless and waterless with the exception of boiling springs, which bubbled up in the most unexpected places. Birds there were none, save a species of lonely snake killers, which half run and half fly over desert spots, and make war upon every reptile and serpent they meet. Having traveled with great difficulty, owing to the treacherous character of the encrusted ground, for about twenty miles, they reached a scene which had probably never before been witnessed by civilized or semi-civilized eyes.

But there it was, and the report of the robbers with regard to it has since been abundantly confirmed. It was simply a huge mountain, as, compared with the surrounding objects, rising say some fifteen hundred feet in height and terribly excoriated, if we may so use the term, by the demon of fire. Like a vulgar monster, sick at its stomach, it continually vomited forth from numbers of mouths large volumes of mud and steam; a regular mud volcano; and, in its belchings, it sent forth different colors of mud—scarlet, yellow and indigo, which, thick and glutinous, rolled down its sides and hardened.

Near its base there was an opening which they had not at first observed, it being on the opposite side, which revealed a tremendous boiling pool, forty feet long by twenty feet wide, and reaching down into cavernous depths from which low rumblings came up like muttered thunder. The ground was hot for a mile around this mud monster, and all the small peaks adjacent were heated. This region, so apochryphal then, has since been thoroughly explored, and the celebrated "Silver Mountain" of the Coso mines lies to the north of the spot described, about twenty-five miles.

On the edge of the big cauldron above named the party saw tracks of naked feet, and the bones of rabbits, "and such small deer," which had been apparently cooked on the heated rocks that form the rim of the cavern. There was, doubtless, a tribe of people somewhere in the vicinity who adopted this unique mode of converting the sublime and terrible into the useful. Following the tracks over the crispy ground, and circling the bed of an extensive lagoon, now dry, they reached a footpath and descended suddenly, and with a transition truly wonderful, into an exceedingly beautiful valley; and here was an Indian village.

The inhabitants were entirely naked, men, women and children, of pigmy size, very dirty, and altogether a very inferior specimen of the sufficiently inferior Root Digger race of California. This tribe live on lizards, crickets, roots and worms, fish and occasional rabbits which they snare. Giving these poor creatures a few presents, the bandits passed on in the path which led through the village, and reaching the pine-clad spurs of the eastern slope, were gratified with the sight of what is now known as Owen's Lake, a body of water filling a huge basin scooped out for it in the elevated land. It is forty miles long and from five to ten miles wide. The waters are clear and brackish, and abound in fish. On one of the streams putting into this lake the robbers fixed their camp.

They were supplied with fish by the Indians, and hunters of the party brought from the hills, not unfrequently, hams of deer and antelope. Here the robbers rested and luxuriated, converting the Indians into servants, laughing at their oddities, and riding or strolling around at their pleasure. In one of his excursions out into the weird realm, upon whose confines he was quartered, Joaquin noticed on a wall of cliffs sculptured figures, of life size, of men and animals.

They appeared to be ancient, and rude as they were, were certainly above any art in the possession of the miserable race then living in those parts. He also found, in an obscure crevice, a rough earthern pot, in which a horned frog had taken up his abode. For how many centuries he had lived there, a venerable hermit, it would be hard to tell. Similar earthen pots have since been found in the neighborhood, and ancient burial places are visible, with circular mounds of stones heaped upon them, about ten feet in diameter, and mouldy with time.

VII

The Banditti Leave Their Resting Place—Indian Guide—Arrive At Tulare River—Valenzuela Despatched on a Special Mission—Reyes Feliz Hung—Anguish of Rosia—Fate of Carmelita—Desperate Conflict Between the Robbers and a Pursuing Party—José Ramune Carrejo's Rancho a Harboring Place for Joaquin—Capture and Execution of Mountain Jim—Messenger Sent to Valenzuela—Robbery Near Dead Man's Creek—Terror of a Chinaman—The Robbers Go Into San Joaquin County—Generosity of Murieta

In this locality, described in the last chapter, the banditti remained until the end of the month of September, when they obtained an Indian guide to lead them through the mountain passes of that quarter, over to the western slope of the Sierra Nevada. The guide took them through a broken mass of volcanic ground to a deep gorge, now known as Copper Cañon.

The passage is only wide enough, in many places, for a man to ride through, and the rocks tower up on each side to a height of three hundred feet. Thence he led them through some rugged mountain spurs into the Mescal Valley. Thence to another patch of crisped and blackened soil into a second lovely valley, whose name I have forgotten, but which is five miles long and well watered; thence over a gradual rise, into Kern Pass; thence down the western slope of the Sierra Nevada; thence along the low, wooded foot-hills that skirt the Tulare River. Here they were within sixty miles of the little town of Visalia, and here, they being then well acquainted with the country, the guide left them.

From this point Joaquin despatched Valenzuela to the Arroyo Cantoova, there to make encampment and collect herds of horses. He himself with Claudio, Three-Fingered Jack and the rest of the band, struck over into San Luis Obispo County, with fifty followers he rested at the Mission of San Luis Obispo, where he recounted the adventures related in the preceding chapter. A portion of his band in a short time went over and stopped at Santa Margarita, about fifteen or twenty miles distant. There were persons connected with both of these extensive ranchos who knew more about Joaquin's concerns than they cared to acknowledge.

While at San Luis Obispo, Joaquin one day took up the Los Angeles *Star*, and was reading the news, when his sight seemed suddenly blasted, and he let the paper fall from his hands.

His affrighted mistress sprang to his side, and clasping his hands, begged him to tell what was the matter. He shook his head for a moment, and the tears gushed from his eyes—aye, robber as he was—as he exclaimed, with quivering lips:

"Rosita, you will never see your brother again. Reyes Feliz is dead. He was hung two days ago by the people of Los Angeles."

Pierced with anguish, the fair girl sunk upon his bosom, and from her dark eyes, overshadowed by the rich, luxuriant hair, which fell around her like a midnight cloud, the storm of her grief poured itself forth in fast and burning drops, which fell like molten lead upon her lover's heart. Why should I describe it? It is well that woman should, like a weeping angel, sanctify our dark and suffering world with her tears. Let them flow. The blood which stains the fair face of our mother Earth may not be washed out with an ocean of tears.

It was indeed true that Reyes Feliz, in his seventeenth year, had met with what is almost always the outlaw's fate—an ignominious death upon the gallows. Having recovered from his wounds, he left San Gabriel and went down to Los Angeles, attended by his faithful Carmelita, where he had been only a few days before he was recognized by an American as one of a party who had once robbed him in the vicinity of Mokelumne Hill. Standing without the least suspicion of danger, in a "fandango house" at Los Angeles, he was suddenly arrested and covered, with irons; he was charged with being a party to the assassination of General Bean, and although no evidence appeared to implicate him in this transaction, yet enough was elicited to show that he was undoubtedly a thief and a murderer.

He was accordingly taken to the gallows, where he kissed the crucifix and made oath that he was innocent of the murder of General Bean, but guilty in many other instances. Though doomed to die at so early an age; young, healthy and full of the fine spirits which give a charm to early manhood; beloved as men are seldom loved; a wild untameable boy; he quailed not in the presence of death, but faced it with a calm brow and tranquil smile. There came over him no shudder or paleness as the rope was adjusted around his neck, and he himself leaped from the platform just as it was about to fall from under him. Alas, for the unfortunate Carmelita!

She wandered alone in the woods, weeping and tearing her hair, and many a startled ear caught the wail of her voice at midnight in the forest. She fled at the approach of a human footstep, but at last they found her cold and ghastly form stretched on a barren rock, in the still beauty of death. The Mexicans buried her by the side of her well beloved Feliz, and the winds shall whisper as mournfully over their graves, as if the purest and best of mortal dust reposed below. All-loving Nature is no respecter of persons, and takes to her bosom all her children, when they have ceased their wanderings, and eases their heartaches in her embracing arms. We may go down to our graves with the scorn of an indignant world upon us, which hurls us from its presence—but the eternal God allows no fragment of our souls, no atom of our dust, to be lost from our universe. Poised on our own immortality, we may defy the human race and all that exists beneath the throne of God!

A few days after the distressing news which they had heard, Joaquin and his sweet Rosita were sitting in front of an old building at the Mission, enjoying, as well as they could, the cool of the evening—for the month of November was still pleasant in the southern counties—when a Mexican rode up on a gallop, and hastily dismounted. He advanced toward Joaquin, who rose at his approach and, seeing that he was a stranger, gave him the secret sign by which any member of the organization might recognize another, though they had never met. It was satisfactorily returned, and the stranger immediately inquired for Joaquin, and expressed a wish to see him. He was of course informed that he was addressing that individual himself, whereupon he proceeded to unfold the object of his mission.

"I am," said he, "most worthy Senor, deputed by a person whom you wot of, residing *near* the rancho of Gen. Pio Pico, to say to you that there is danger where you now are. A party of Americans, well armed and mounted, have passed the rancho Los Coyotes in this direction, and it is no doubt their intention to surprise you at your present retreat. I myself passed them this morning, without being perceived, encamped about fifteen miles from this place, and I seriously believe that you had better look out."

"Very well," replied the chief, without changing countenance, "this is as good as I want; hold yourself in readiness to serve me as a guide to their encampment, for I intend to surprise *them*."

Summoning Three-Fingered Jack and Claudio, he informed them of the facts which he had heard, and of his intentions, directing them to prepare the band immediately for action. In an hour afterwards the different members came galloping up from various parts of the rancho, booted, spurred and equipped in brilliant style, to the number of forty-five men. They were fine looking fellows, and scarcely any of them over thirty-five years of age. Under the guide of the Los Coyotes messenger, who was furnished with a fresh horse, they started just as night set in upon their dangerous expedition.

After a ride of two hours and a half they arrived at their destination. The fires were still burning, but the camp was abandoned. It was too dark to follow a trail, and they stopped for the night. At daybreak they arose, 'mounted their horses and pursued a very fresh trail which led through the woods, as if carefully to avoid the main roads. By the number of tracks it was evident that they were in pursuit of a strong force. The trail led precisely in the course of San Luis Obispo, and it was apparent that the Americans had started for that place about the same time that Joaquin had left it; but he having traveled the main road, thus missed them on the way.

Arriving at ten o'clock within two miles of the Mission, he halted and sent a spy forward to examine and report, who returned in a short time with the information that the party, consisting of fifty men, had left the Mission at daylight on that morning, with the evident purpose of taking the beaten road straight back to their encampment of the day before, the tracks of the banditti being still fresh on the ground. It was plain therefore, that finding unmistakable indications that the bandits had stayed at their encampment, and had followed their trail toward the Mission, they would hurry on to overtake them, and would be able to make the entire circuit before sundown of that day. The young chief clapped his hands together in perfect glee.

"We have them boys! we have got them *dead*!"

He wheeled his horse directly around, and led his company about three miles back on the trail which they had just come, and halted at the junction of two deep gulches, rugged and shaggy with overhanging rocks. Directing his men to hide their horses at a distance of three or four hundred yards from the trail, he ordered them next to conceal themselves in the nooks and crevices of the surrounding bluffs. They lay there as still as death for about two hours, when the clatter of horses feet was heard distinctly in the distance. Nearer and nearer they dame, and in a few minutes a fine looking young man, with blue eyes and light hair, rode up within twenty yards of Joaquin, followed by about, fifty other Americans, armed with rifles and revolvers.

"I don't like the looks of this place at all," said the young man, and hardly had the words escaped his lips, before the rocks blazed around him, and the sharp reports of twenty or thirty pistols rang in his ears. His hat was shot from his head, and his horse fell under him. A dozen of his followers bit the dust.

"Dismount, boys, aid scale the rocks! Give them no advantage Face them in their very teeth! It is our only chance."

They sprang to the rocks at the word, each man to the quarter which he chose, and hand to hand bearded their hidden foes in their dens. It could scarcely be called a battle between two distinct forces; it was rather a number of separate single combats, in which nothing could avail a man but his own right arm and dauntless heart. Joaquin sprang from his hiding place to have a freer sweep of his arm, when he met at the very threshold the young Anglo Saxon. A flash of recognition passed between them, and Joaquin turned as if to leap upon a rock at his right, but at the moment that his antagonist jumped in that direction to intercept the movement, he wheeled to the left, and throwing out his foot with a sudden and vigorous stroke, knocked the young man's heels from under him, and he fell with violence upon his face.

Before he could rise, the wily bandit leaped upon him like a panther, and sheathed his knife in his heart. It was too sad, but as I have said before, an invisible guardian fiend pursued everywhere this extraordinary man. Having no time to repeat the blow, especially as it seemed unnecessary, he drew forth the dripping blade, and rushed to another scene of the conflict. He was met at almost every step, and fought his way like a tiger, gashed and bleeding, but still strong and unfainting. Dead men lay upon every side, both Americans and Mexicans, and in front of Three-Fingered Jack were stretched five men, with their skulls broken by the butt end of his revolver, which he had used as a club after emptying its contents, and at the moment that Joaquin's eye met him, he was stooping, with glaring eyes and a hideous smile, over a prostrate American, in whose long hair he had wound his left hand, and across whose throat he was drawing the coarse-grained steel of his huge home-made bowie knife.

With a shout of delight he severed the neck joint and threw the gaping head over the rocks. He was crazy with the sight of blood, and searched eagerly for another victim. He scarcely knew his leader, and the latter had called to him three times before he recovered his senses.

"Ah, Murieta," said he, smacking his lips, "this has been a great day. Damn 'em! How my knife lapped up their blood."

The fight now having lasted half an hour, and there being no prospect that either party would conquer, so equally were they matched, it gradually subsided, and each side gradually drew off from the other, with a tacit understanding that they were mutually satisfied to cry quits. Joaquin looked around and saw that he had lost twenty men, among whom was the invaluable Claudio, and ascertained the loss of his enemies to be very near the same, perhaps a little over. Mounting their horses, the bandits rode off in silence toward San Luis Obispo, while the surviving Americans found as many of their horses as had not left them during the conflict, and retired to their homes in Santa Barbara County, having made arrangements on the way for the burial of their deceased comrades. During the following night a company from the Mission went over to the bloody scene with picks and shovels, and buried the dead bodies of the bandits near the spot where they fell. On the next morning Joaquin summoned the Los Coyotes messenger, and said to him:

"Go back and tell my friend, who sent you, that the danger is passed, and hand him this purse. For yourself, take this one," handing him another well-filled bag.

Attention having being attracted to the San Luis Obispo rancho, the bandit thought it prudent to go elsewhere. Accordingly word was sent over to their friends who were rusticating at Santa Margarita, to join them, and they forth with started to a well known harboring place not more than a *thousand miles* from José Ramune Carrejo's rancho. Here they remained until such as were wounded recovered their usual health and strength—and here, again, Joaquin heard news similar to that which shocked him at San Luis Obispo, namely, that Mountain Jim had been hung at San Diego. This misfortune happened to the jolly robber from his own carelessness. He and Valenzuela had stopped at a drinking shop on the San Diego River, some, fifteen or twenty miles from the bay of that name, and had taken a glass of execrable brandy, when a party of four or five Americans rode up and alighted, who looked so very suspiciously at Valenzuela and partner, that the former took his friend out, and told him that it was his opinion they both had better leave as quick as possible.

Mountain Jim was under the influence of liquor, and laughing at what he those to term the silly fears of Valenzuela, he went back into the house swearing and swaggering. Pretty soon after, a' dozen more Americans approached on horseback, seeing whom, Valenzuela mounted into his saddle and called to Jim to come along. But Jim only laughed, and took another glass of liquor.

"Curse the fool!" muttered the bandit, "he will be the death of both of us. For my part, I will keep my own distance from those scurvy looking fellows, at any rate."

The new party no sooner arrived than they rushed up to the door of the drinking house and drew their revolvers—a scuffle ensued inside, and Valenzuela, well aware of what was going on, and that it was useless to contend against such great odds, merely fired one shot into the crowd at the door, which took effect in the abdomen of one of the party, and wheeling his horse broke off like a thunderbolt. Several of the Americans pursued him, but his fine, swift animal distanced them so far, that they might as well have attempted to catch the red-winged spirit of a storm. Poor Mountain Jim! He was never destined to tread the mountains again. He was taken to the town of San Diego, and hung with as little ceremony as if he had been a dog. Well fitted was he to grace a gallows, for his merits certainly entitled him to a distinguished elevation.

From his present stopping place Joaquin sent a messenger, about the first of December, to the Arroyo Cantoova, to see Valenzuela, if he was there, and if he was absent to await his return, in order to inform him that it was made his duty to continue the business in which he was engaged, through the entire winter, or until such time as Joaquin should arrive at the rendezvous. The messenger returned after a few days and stated that, he had found Valenzuela and band at the Arroyo, with tents pitched, and a herd of fine horses amounting to between five and six hundred, feeding on the pasture, and that the bold leader had, signified a willing obedience to his chiefs mandate.

"He is a glorious fellow," exclaimed Joaquin. "He didn't practice under that hardened old priest, Jurata, without learning something."

Spies were now ranging the country every day, picking up valuable information; and among other things, it was ascertained that an, opinion prevailed that Joaquin had gone to the State of Sonora. Thinking it a favorable time, he issued forth with his whole force, uniting, Three-Fingered Jack's party with Claudio's, which last was now under the leadership of a member of the band named Reis—and started up into Mariposa County for the purpose of plunder.

On the road that leads from Dead Mai's Creek to the Merced River, he met four Frenchmen, six Germans and three Americans, walking and driving mules before them, packed with provisions, blankets and mining utensils. Having so large a party with him, numbering about thirty men, he had no difficulty in stopping the travelers as long as he wished to detain them. His men stood around with pistols cocked, while Joaquin dismounted, and walking up to a terrified Frenchman, who was armed with a revolver which he was afraid to use, took him by the top of his head, and jerked him around once or twice, slapped him across the face with his open hand, and told him to "shell out."

The French-man hauled out a well-filled purse and was handing it over, when others of his companions made a show to draw their pistols and defend their gold dust. The robbers were too quick for them, and more than half of the unfortunate miners were shot down in their tracks. Joaquin brandished his glittering blade in the faces of the survivors, and threatened to cut every one of their windpipes if they didn't hand out "what little loose change" they had about them, in half a minute! His polite request was complied with, and the little loose change amounted to about $15,000. He then bestowed a kick or two on some of the number as a parting tribute of regard, and told them to "roll on." Three-Fingered Jack insisted on killing the whole company, but the chief overruled him.

Riding forward after this transaction, they had not gone more than two miles when they met a Chinaman with a long tall, carrying a large bundle suspended at each end of a stick laid across his shoulders, walking leisurely along with his head bent to the ground. Looking up and seeing so large a number of armed men before him, his eyes rolled in sudden fear, and he ducked his half shaved head in unmistakable homage and respect to—the revolvers and bowie knives which met his vision. No one harmed him, and he shuffled on vastly gratified and relieved.

He had passed only a few minutes when he was heard howling and screaming in the most harrowing manner; and looking back they discovered the horrified Celestial, with his tail flying in the wind, running toward them at the top of his speed; with arms sawing the air, and bundle *less*, while the ground clattered under his wooden shoes; and just behind him, with blazing eyes, and his huge home-made knife 'in his right hand, appeared Three-Fingered Jack, who had stopped at a spring and was tying his horse to a bush at the moment that the Chinaman came up. It was too good an opportunity to be lost, and he darted like a wild hyena at the astounded Oriental, who applied himself to his heels with the utmost vigor that he could command.

Joaquin bowed himself upon the saddle in a convulsion of laughter at the ridiculous appearance of the Chinaman, but speedily confronted Jack and told him to stop. Woh Le fell upon his knees in deepest adoration of his preserver. Joaquin bade him go on his way, and laughingly reprimanded Jack for wanting to kill so pitiful a looking creature.

"Well," said Jack, "I can't help it; but, somehow or other, I love to smell the blood of a Chinaman. Besides, it's such easy work to kill them. It's a kind of luxury to cut their throats."

Proceeding across the woods and mountains, the banditti in a few days struck the main road leading from the town of Mariposa to Stockton, in San Joaquin county. Robbing once in a while as they went along, they arrived late one night at a ferry on the Tuolumne River, Tuolumne county, and finding the boat locked to the shore so that they could not exercise the privilege of crossing themselves which was their usual custom, they rode up to the ferryman's house, and very nearly beat the door down before they could arouse him. He came out at last with a terrified look, and asked what they wanted.

"We want to cross the river," replied Joaquin; "and before doing so we wish to obtain from you the loan of what spare cash you may have about you. You have the best evidence of the urgency of our request," cocking his pistol and presenting it close to the fellow's head.

"Never mind the evidence, Señor; I believe you without it. I will certainly loan you all I have got."

So saying, he lighted a candle and got out a purse from under his pillow, containing a hundred dollars.

"Come," said Jack, bursting a cap at his head, "you have got more; and was cocking his pistol for another trial, when Joaquin very fiercely told him to know his place. Turning to the trembling ferryman he said: "Is this all you have got?"

"Precisely all, Señor; but you are welcome to it."

"I won't take it," said the young chief, with a flush of pride; "you are a poor man and never injured me. Put us over the river and I will pay you for your trouble."

I mention this incident merely to show that Murieta in his worst days had yet a remnant of that noble spirit which had been his original nature, and to correct those who have said that he was lost to every generous sentiment.

VIII

Arrival at Stockton—Joaquin Rides Boldly Through the City—Daring Attack On a Schooner in the Slough—Depature for Arroyo Cantoova—Happy Reunion of the Bandits—Joaquin Reveals His Future Plans—Guerra's Wife Becomes Restive—American Hunters Fall Into a Trap—How They Got Out of It

The party arrived in the neighborhood of Stockton after two days' travel, and camped on the plain, under an oak grove, about three miles from that city. They were seen at their encampment, but not suspected. Indeed it was then, as it is now, so common a thing to see companies of men engaged in the various occupations of packers, cattle drovers, horse traders, hunters and the like, stationed by the banks of some cool stream, or resting under the shade of trees at a distance from any house, or with their tents pitched in some lonely place for weeks at a time that it was scarcely just to suspect a party to be criminal, merely from circumstances like these.

The knowledge of everybody that it was the habit among all classes to go armed and to camp out, in every sort of a place, materially aided the banditti in their movements, for it gave them the opportunity to remain perfectly safe until they chose to avow their real characters by some open outrage and villainy.

One fine Sunday morning, while the bells were ringing for church in the goodly city of Stockton, and well-dressed gentlemen were standing at the corners of the streets, marking with critical eyes the glancing feet and the flaunting dresses of the ladies who swept by them in the halo of beauty and perfumery, a fine looking man whom they had never seen before—having long, black hair hanging over his shoulders, and a piercing black eye—rode through the streets, carelessly looking at the different, objects which happened to attract his attention. So finely was he dressed, and so superbly was his horse comparisoned, that without seeming to know it, he was the observed of all observers.

"What a splendid looking fellow!" observed the ladies.

"He must be a young Mexican grandee, at least, on a journey of pleasure," said one.

"I think," said another, "it must be Gen. Vallejo's son."

"I don't believe lie has any," said a third; and they became so much interested in their conjectures about the young man that it is doubtful whether they paid much attention to the very prosy minister who was then acting as the "bright and shining light" amidst the surrounding darkness.

The youthful cavalier, after attracting uncommon attention, by riding over the city, finally stopped at the side of a house, upon which were posted several notices—one reading as follows-:

"For Sail.

> the surscribur ophfers for sail a yaulbote hicht at the hed of the Slew terms cash or kabbige turnips and sich like will bea tayken."

To which fine specimen of polite literature was appended the name of a worthy citizen, who was then fishing for his living, but has since been fishing for various distinguished offices in that county.

Another one was a "notis" that some person either wanted to hire some one else, or *be* hired himself, as a cook—it was impossible to tell which.

A third was an auctioneer's notice.

> "Honor before the 25 da of Dec I will offur to the hiest bider a brown mule ate yeer old, a gilding 16 hans hi, and a span of jacks consistin of long years and a good voyce."

I have a notion to publish the name signed to this rare advertisement, especially as the auctioneer seems to have been something of a wag as well as ignoramus. But, perhaps, it will be better not. A fourth was headed, in good English, and a fair running hand.

"Five Thousand Dollars Reward for Joaquin—dead or alive."

And stated that the citizens of San Joaquin county offered that amount for the apprehension or the killing of that noted robber.

Seeing this, the young Mexican dismounted, and taking out his pencil, wrote something underneath, and leisurely rode out of town.

No less than a dozen persons, stimulated by curiosity, went to the paper to see what was written, when they read the following in pencil:

*"I will give $10,000. Joaquin."
*See newspapers of that period.

Numerous were the exclamations of astonishment at this discovery, and nothing else was talked of for a week, among the ladies at least, who got hold of the fact almost before it was discovered, and insisted each to the other that they had remarked that the young man had a peculiarly wild and terrible look, and they had suspected very strongly though they had never mentioned it to any one, that it was none other than the noted personage whom it proved to be.

Joaquin appeared on this occasion in his real features. He frequently went afterwards, however, into that city completely disguised, and learned many things important for him to hear. Ascertaining one evening that a schooner would go down the slough in a few hours, bound for San Francisco, on board of which were two miners from San Andreas, in Calaveras county, with heavy bags of gold dust, who designed to take their departure for the States, he took three of his men who were lounging around town, with him, and jumping into a skiff shot down the slough, and tying up his boat in a bend of the water, hid in the *tules* and patiently waited for the schooner to come along.

The mosquitoes bit him unmercifully, and he was almost tempted to abandon the enterprise on their account; but the prospect of so good a haul was, on reflection, not to be resisted. He cursed himself for not bringing some matches with which he might have kindled a fire, and sought the protection of its smoke; but perseverance is always rewarded, if the object desired lies in the bounds of possibility, and waiting like a martyr for three mortal hours, in those *tules*, which are a perfect "mosquito kingdom," where huge gallinippers reign as the aristocracy, he at last saw the white sheeted schooner stealing along in the crooks and turns of *just the crookedest stream in the whole world*, so narrow and so completely hid in its windings by the tall flags which overspread the plains for many miles to the right and left that the white sail looked like a ghost gliding along over the waving grass.

As the vessel came opposite, Joaquin and companions shoved their boat out into the stream, and tying it to the schooner's side, leaped on board of her, and commenced firing without saying a word. They shot down the two young men who managed the vessel before they had time, to use their double-barreled shot-guns, which they always carried for the purpose of shooting water-fowl in the slough and up the San Joaquin River, and rushing aft attacked the two miners, who had risen at the the report of the pistols, and were standing with their revolvers drawn and cocked, ready for action.

They and the robbers fired simultaneously.

Two of Joaquin's men fell dead on the deck, and the miners fell at the same time. Their wallets were soon stripped from them by Joaquin and his surviving companion, and finding some matches, they set fire to the vessel, and left her to burn down. They rowed their skiff to the head of the slough in Stockton, and wended their way back to their encampment. Ere daylight there was no trace of murder on the slough, but a dark hulk which was hardly visible on the water's edge. By this operation Joaquin realized twenty thousand dollars. Having now between forty and fifty thousand dollars in gold dust, he ordered his bands to pack up, and started for the rendezvous of Arroyo Cantoova, passing by José Ramune Carrejo's rancho, and taking the lovely Rosita along with him, who had been staying there during his trip to Stockton.

He reached the Arroyo about the middle of the day, and it was a beautiful sight that, met his eye as he gazed over the extensive valley, and saw a thousand fine horses feeding on the rich grass, or galloping, with flowing manes and expanded nostrils, in graceful circles over the plain.

"Valenzuela has done his work well," said the elated chief, "ten times better than I had expected he would."

Seeing one of his herdsmen looking at him a short distance off as if endeavoring to recognize him, he rode up to him and asked him in reference to Valenzuela.

"He has been gone," said the vaquero, "about a week—we expect him every day."

The newly arrived party then rode up to the tents under the trees, and dismounted. The busy cooks hurried up the fires, and the fresh venison and bear meat was soon smoking on the irons, and emitting a most delicious savor, such as tempts the appetite of a hardy mountaineer. Broiled quails and grouse, sweet and oily, the latter of which had been brought from the tall spruce trees at a height of three hundred feet, by the long maple-stocked and silver-mounted rifles which stood at the corner of one of the tents, were hanging in front of the blaze, suspended by their necks to branching sticks driven into the ground. The hot coffee steamed up from the large pot with a most stimulating effect; everything was spread forth in superabundance, scattered over a large white cloth that covered a few yards square of green grass, and 'at a signal from the cooks, who were also the waiters, forty fierce and hungry brigands sat down, and with the utmost expedition consistent with respect for their leader, made havoc among the victuals.

Just at this moment a mounted company dashed up at full speed, giving the well known whoop by which they could be recognized as friends, and dismounted. It was Valenzuela and a portion of his band, the remainder of whom soon after came in, driving two hundred and fifty fine American horses before them. The circle was enlarged, the cooks went to work afresh, and soon the whole banditti were seated at the ample banquet. Generous wines stood sparkling, in their midst, with which scarcely any refused to refresh themselves. Conversation flowed freely, and each one had a tale to tell of hair-breadth escapes and daring deeds.

On the following morning Joaquin collected his bands around him, numbering from a late accession of "fighting members," as he called them, one hundred men, and explained to them fully his views and purposes.

He informed them that he could command, if he desired, in all two thousand men who were ready to organize in Sonora, Lower California, and in this State, that he had money in abundance deposited in a safe place, meaning with his secret partner in Sonora; that he intended to arm and equip and make a clean sweep of the southern counties; that he intended to kill the Americans by wholesale, burn their ranchos and run off their property, at one single swoop, so rapidly that they would not have time to collect an opposing force before he would have finished the work and found safety in the mountains of Sonora; that when he had done this he would wind up his career, divide his substance with the band now attending him, and spend the rest of his days in peace; that he was now preparing for this grand climax, and that this was the reason that he had been so steadily collecting horses.

These avowals leaked out through persons not sufficiently reticent on the ranches in the habit of harboring Joaquin, and came to the ears of Captain Harry Love, whom we have before mentioned, and others, causing them to use renewed exertions to capture or slay the daring robber.

The banditti shouted in loud applause of their gallant leader. Their eyes kindled with enthusiasm at the magnificent prospect which he presented to them, and they could scarcely contain themselves in view of the astounding revelations which he had made. They had entertained no adequate idea of the splendid genius which belonged to their chief, although they had loved and admired him throughout his dangerous career, they were fired with new energy, and more than ever willing and anxious to obey him at all hazards, and under the most disadvantageous circumstances.

On this same day he dispatched a remittance of $50,000 to his secret partner in Sonora, under a strong force commanded by Valenzuela, and directed Three-Fingered Jack, with fifty men, to drive off to the same State a thousand head of the horses which had been collected. Joaquin was accordingly left at the rendezvous, with twenty-five men, who had nothing to do but kill game, and attend to their horses, and clean their arms.

The widow of Gonzalez, and present wife of the brute Guerra, who looked more like a grizzly bear than a human being, wished to go off with Three-Fingered Jack, but Guerra begged his brother bandit, of whom he was afraid, so hard to leave her with him that Jack forced her to stay. Guerra was by no means so kind to her as Gonzalez had been, and one night while he was asleep she was about to cut his throat, when Joaquin, who was lying in the same tent fiercely told her to behave herself, and assured her with an emphasis that he would hold her responsible if Guerra was ever found dead about camp. She threw her knife spitefully toward Joaquin and laid down again by her adorable spouse, who snored in blissful ignorance of his wife's affectionate purpose.

Lounging in his tent one misty day—for the rainy season had set in—Joaquin was aroused from the luxurious lap of his mistress by one of his sentinels, who galloped up and informed him that he had just discovered a fresh trail through the grass, about a mile and a half below on the Cantoova Creek, and from appearances he should judge there were eight or ten men. It was important to keep a sharp lookout, and to allow no Americans to leave that valley with the knowledge that it was occupied by any body of men whatever, as such a circumstance would materially interfere with the gigantic plans projected. Accordingly, it was not long before Joaquin was mounted upon one of his swiftest horses and accompanied by fifteen picked men. They proceeded to the trail indicated by the sentinel and rode rapidly for two hours, which brought them in sight of ten Americans, who halted in curious surprise and waited for them to come up.

"Who are you?" said Joaquin, "and what is your business in these parts?"

They replied that they were hunters in search of bears and deer.

"We are hunters, also," rejoined the bandit, "and are camped just across the plain here. Come over with us, and let us have a chat. Besides, we have some first rate liquor at our camp."

Suspecting nothing wrong, the hunters accompanied them, and having dismounted at the tents and turned out their horses to graze, found themselves suddenly in a very doubtful position. They were surrounded by a company more than double their own, who made demonstrations not at all grateful to their sight, and in a few moments they realized the bitter fact that they were driven to the extremity of a hopeless struggle for their lives. They remonstrated with Joaquin against so shameless an act as the cold-blooded murder of men who had never injured him.

"You have found me here," he replied, "and I have no guarantee that you will not betray me. If I do not tell you who I am, you will think it no harm to say you have seen a man of my description; and if I do tell you, then you will be certain to mention it at the first opportunity."

At this moment a young man, originally from the wilds of Arkansas, not more than eighteen years of age, advanced in front of his trembling comrades, and standing face to face with the robber chief, addressed him in a firm voice to the following effect:

"I suspect strongly who you are, sir. I am satisfied that you are Joaquín Murieta. I am also satisfied that you are a brave man, who would not unnecessarily commit murder. You would not wish to take our lives unless your own safety I demanded it. I do not blame you, following the business you do, for desiring to put an effectual seal of silence on our tongues. But listen to me just a moment. You see that I am no coward. I do not look at you with the aspect of a man, who would tell a falsehood to save his life. I promise you faithfully for myself, and in behalf of my companions, that if you spare our lives, which are completely in your power, not a word shall be breathed of your whereabouts. I will myself kill the first man who says a word in regard to it. Under different circumstances I should take a different course, but *now*, I am conscious that to spare our lives, it will be an act of magnanimity on your part, and I stake my honor, not as an American citizen, but as a man, who is simply bound by justice to himself, under circumstances in which no other considerations can prevail, that you shall not be betrayed. If you say you will spare us, we thank you. If you say no, we can only fight till we die, and you must lose some of your lives in the conflict."

Joaquin drew his hand across his brow, and looked thoughtful, and undecided. A beautiful female approached him from the tent near by, and touched him on the shoulder.

"Spare them, Joaquin," she tremulously whispered, and looking at him with pleading eyes, retired softly to her seat again.

Raising his fine head with a lofty look, he bent his large clear eyes upon the young American as if he would read him like an outspread page. He answered his glance with a look so royally sincere that Joaquin exclaimed with sudden energy:

"I will spare you. Your countrymen have injured me; they have made me what I am, but I scorn to take the advantage of so brave a man. I will risk a look and voice like yours, if it should lead to perdition. Saddle their horses for them," he said to his followers, "and let them depart in peace."

The party were very soon mounted again, and showering blessings on Joaquin, who had become suddenly transformed into an angel in their estimation, they took their leave. I have never learned that the young man, or any of his party, broke their singular compact, and indeed it seems to me that it would have been very questionable morality in them to have done so, for certainly, however much they owed to society, it would have been a suicidal act to refuse to enter into such an agreement, and as nothing but a firm conviction that they intended to keep their word, could have induced Joaquin to run so great a risk, they were bound to preserve their faith inviolate.

If they had a right to purchase their lives at the price of silence, they had an equal right, and not only that, but were morally bound to stand up to their bargain. It would be well if men were never forced into such a position, but society has no right, after it has happened, to wring from them a secret which belongs to *them*, and not to the world. In such matters God is the only judge.

IX

Arrivals from Sonora—The Mysterious Death of Guerra—Operations in Calaveras County—Hair Breadth Escape of Joaquin

The month of December was drawing to a close, and the busy brain of the accomplished chief had mapped out the full plan of his operations for a new year just at hand. It was the year which would close his short and tragical career with a crowning glory,—a deed of daring and of power, which would redeem with its refulgent light the darkness of his previous history, and show him to after times not as a mere outlaw, committing petty depredations and robberies, but as a *hero* who has revenged his country's wrongs, and washed, out her disgrace in the blood of her enemies.

It was time for Three-Fingered Jack and Valenzuela to return from Sonora, and he waited patiently for their arrival, in order to replenish his purse largely during the first months of the new year, so that he might execute his magnificent purpose without embarrassment or obstruction. In a few days Garcia and Valenzuela returned, accompanied by an old guerrilla comrade of the latter, named Luis Vulvia.

The two had lost five men from their bands, killed in several skirmishes, on their way back, with the citizens of Los Angeles county. Further than this they had received no injury, and were in fine health and spirits, although their horses were somewhat jaded. Each leader handed to Joaquin a well-filled purse of gold coin. Having rested two days, the major portion of the banditti mounted fresh horses, and leaving the remainder, numbering twenty-five men, at the rendezvous, under the command of Guerra, with whom they also left the females, not thinking it prudent, in view of the bloody scenes which would be enacted, to take them along, they set out for Calaveras county.

They had not been gone more than three days before a quarrel arose between Guerra and his affectionate wife, which ended in his giving her a wholesome thrashing. She submitted to the infliction with great apparent humility, but the next morning at breakfast time, when Guerra was called and did not come, several of his companions went into his tent to arouse him and found him stone dead. There was no sign of violence on his body, and it remained a complete mystery how he died. He had been a hard drinker, and finally his death was attributed to an over-indulgence the night before. But the fact of the case was, that the unconscious sleeper had received at midnight just one drop of molten lead into his ear, tipped from a ladle by a small and skillful hand. Byron has said in one of his misanthropic verses:

"Woman's tears produced at will,
Deceive in life, unman in death,"

and the truth of this bitter asseveration was partially illustrated when the inconsolable widow wept so long and well over the husband, whom she like a second, nay the thousandth Jezebel, had made a corpse. It is barely possible, however, that her tears were those of remorse. She accepted for her third husband a young fellow in the band at the rendezvous, named Isidora Conejo, who loved her much more tenderly than did the brutal Guerra, whom she so skillfully put out of the way. This young man was a few years her junior, but she looked as youthful as himself.

Twice widowed, her sorrows had not dimmed the lustre of her eyes, or taken the gloss from her rich dark hair, or the rose from her cheeks. Her step was as buoyant as ever, the play of her limbs as graceful, the heave of her impulsive bosom as entrancing and her voice as full of music, as if she had never lost Gonzalez or murdered Guerra. There are some women who seem never to grow old. As each successive spring renews the plumage of the birds, so with them the passing years add fresh beauty to their forms, and decay long lingers ere he has the heart to touch their transcendent loveliness with his cold and withering fingers. The fascinating Margarita was one of these.

Joaquin with his party, fully bent on the most extensive mischief, reentered Calaveras county about the middle of December. This county was then, as it is now, one of the richest in the State of California. Its mountains were veined with gold—the beds of its clear and far-rushing streams concealed the yellow grains in abundance—and the large quartz leads, like the golden tree of the Hesperides, spread their fruitful branches abroad through the hills. Its fertile valleys bloomed with voluptuous flowers, over which you might walk as on a carpet woven of rainbows—or waved with the green and yellow harvests, whose reedy music charmed the ear.

The busy wheels of the sawmills, with their glittering teeth, rived the mighty pines which stood like green and spiral towers, one above another, from base to summit of the majestic peaks. Long tunnels, dimly lighted, with swinging lamps or flickering candles, searched far into the bowels of the earth for her hidden secrets. Those which were abandoned served as dens for the cougar and wolf, or, more frequently as the dens of thieves.

Over this attractive field of his enterprises, Joaquin scattered his party in different directions. He entrusted Reis with the command of twenty men; Luis. Vulvia with that of twenty-five, retaining about fifteen for his own use, among whom was the terrible Three-Fingered Jack, and the no less valuable Valenzuela, and employed the remainder as spies and bearers of news from one point of action to another.

Reis went up to the headwaters of the Stanislaus River, between whose forks the rich valleys, covered with horses, afforded a fine theatre for his operations. On all the mountain-fed branches and springs of these forks, the picks and shovels of thousands of miners were busy, and the industrious Chinese had pitched their little cloth villages in a hundred spots, and each day hurried to and fro like innumerable ants, picking up the small but precious grains. Luis Vulvia—as daring a man as Claudio, and as cunning—proceeded to the headwaters of the Mokelumne River; and detached portions of these two bands, at intervals ranged the intermediate space. Joaquin himself had no particular sphere, but chose his ground according to circumstances. Keeping Three-Fingered Jack with him most of the time, he yet once in a while gave him the charge of a small party, with liberty to do as he pleased—a favor which the bloody monster made good use of, so much so that scarcely a man whom he ever met, rich or poor, escaped with his life.

The horse which this hideous fellow rode might have rivalled "Bucephalus" in breadth of chest, high spirit and strength of limb, united with swiftness. No one but a powerful man could have rode him; but Three-Fingered Jack, with a fine Mexican saddle, (the best saddle in the world) fastened securely with a broad girth made of horse hair, as strong as a band of iron, and curbing him with a huge Spanish bit, with which he might have rent his jaw, managed the royal animal with ease. To see this man, with his large and rugged frame, in which the strength of a dozen common men slumbered, his face and forehead scarred with bullets and grooved with the wrinkles of grim thoughts, and his intensely lighted eyes glaring maliciously, like caverned demons, under his shaggy brows; to see such a man mounted upon a raven-black horse, whose nostrils drew the air like a gust of wind into his broad chest, whose wrathful hoof pawed the ground as if the spirit of his rider inspired him, and whose wild orbs rolled from side to side in untamable fire; would aptly remind one of old Satan himself, mounted upon a hell-born beast, after he had been "let loose for a thousand years."

Among the many thrilling instances of the daring and recklessness of spirit which belonged to Joaquin, there is one which I do not feel at liberty to omit, especially as it comes naturally and properly in this connection. Shortly after he parted from Reis and Luis Vulvia, he went up into the extreme north of the county. There, at the head of a branch of the South Fork of the Mokelumne River, in a wild and desolate region near the boundary line of Calaveras and El Dorado counties, were located a company of miners, consisting of twenty-five men.

They were a long distance from any neighbors, having gone there well armed on a prospecting tour, which resulted in their finding diggings so rich that they were persuaded to pitch their tents and remain. One morning while they were eating their breakfast on a flat rock—a natural table which stood in front of their tents—armed as usual with their revolvers, a young fellow with very dark hair and eyes, rode up and saluted them. He spoke very good English, and they could scarcely make out whether he was a Mexican or an American. They requested him to get down and eat with them, but he politely declined. He sat with one leg crossed over his horse's neck very much at his ease, conversing freely on various subjects, until Jim Boyce, one of the partners, who had been to the spring after water, appeared in sight. At the first glance of him the young horseman flung his reclining leg back over the saddle, and spurred his horse Boyce roared out:

"Boys, that fellow is Joaquin! D—n it, shoot him!" At the same instant he himself fired, but without effect.

Joaquin dashed down to the creek below with headlong speed, and crossed with the intention, no doubt, to escape over the hills, which ran parallel with the stream, but his way was blocked up by perpendicular rocks, and his only practicable path was a narrow digger-trail, which led along the side of a huge mountain, directly over a ledge of rocks a hundred yards in length, which hung beetling over the rushing stream beneath, in a direct line with the hill upon which the miners had pitched their tents, and not more than forty yards distant.

It was a fearful gauntlet for any man to run. Not only was there danger of falling a hundred feet from the rocks, but he must run in a parallel line with his enemies, and in pistol range for a hundred yards. In fair view of him stood the whole company with their revolvers drawn. He dashed along that fearful trail as if he had been mounted on a spirit-steed, shouting as he passed:

"I am Joaquin! Kill me if you can!"

Shot after shot came clanging around his head, and bullet after bullet flattened on the wall of slate at his right. In the midst of the first firing his hat was knocked from his head, and left his long black hair streaming behind him. He had no time to use his own pistol, but knowing that his only chance lay in the swiftness of his sure-footed animal, he drew his keenly polished bowie knife in proud defance of the danger, and waved it in scorn as he rode on. It was perfectly sublime to see such superhuman daring and recklessness. At each report, which came fast and thick, he kissed the flashing blade and waved it at his foes. He passed the ordeal, as awful and harrowing to a man's nerves as can be conceived, untouched by a ball and otherwise unharmed. In a few moments a loud whoop rang out in the woods a quarter of a mile distant, and the bold rider was safe!

X

Jim Boyce and Companions Make Ready and Follow On the Track of Joaquin—Brilliant Stratagem of the Robber Chief—His Ingenious Management in Releasing Luis Vulvia—He Passes Himself Off as S. Harrington, of San Jose—The Quien Sabe Rancho, Munos, and Joaquin Guerra's Rancho Harboring Places for Joawuin Murieta—The Robbers in an Abandoned Tunnel—Love Scene on the South Fork of Stanislaus River, and How it Was Broken in Upon—Girl Abducted By the Robbers—Her Subsequent Fate

Joaquin, knowing well the determined character of Jim Boyce, and deeming it more than probable that he had heard of the different large rewards offered for his capture, or death, amounting to fifteen or twenty thousand dollars, he made up his mind speedily, that an attack would be made upon him by the whole party of miners, if he remained at his encampment, which was some five miles distant from their own. Concluding they could not collect their horses together and prepare their arms and ammunition in a proper manner for an attack or pursuit, before, night, he conceived a plan, the most brilliant and ingenious that ever entered an outlaw's brain, by which to defeat their purposes and carry out his own original intention of robbing them.

Knowing that a trail could very well be made in the night but that it could only be followed in the daytime, he ordered his men, numbering fifteen, to saddle up and make ready for a ride. They obeyed with alacrity, and without question, and in a few minutes were on their horses and ready to move forward. The chief led the way in silence, proceeding over the pine ridges in an easterly direction. He rode on vigorously until night, over very rough ground, having traversed a distance of twenty miles; but wishing to place a still greater distance between him and the Encampment which he had left, he did not come to final halt until a late hour.

Building a huge fire, and hitching their animals near by, the wearied bandits hastily threw their blankets down and stretched their limbs upon them for repose: Sentinels alternately sat up until daylight, so that at the first touch of dawn the whole band arose and again started, having lost only four hours in sleep. They journeyed on in the same course, as briskly as possible until noon, when, having reached a nice little valley, covered with grass and wild clover, and watered by a beautiful spring which bubbled up from the roots of a clump of evergreen oaks, distant about twenty miles from their last encampment, they stopped for two hours to let their horses graze, and to refresh their own rather empty stomachs with the sardines and crackers which they generally carried with them.

Here they left strong indications that they had spent the night, but established the contrary fact by riding on for the remainder of the day, whose close found them at another distance of twenty miles. Building fires as before, and eating a hasty supper they again mounted, and having made a circle of five miles in their course, suddenly turned to the westward, and encamped about three o'clock in the morning at a spot distant another common day's journey from the last starting point. Thus traveling and resting, after the lapse of a few days they found themselves in the original trail upon which they started.

Jim Boyce and company had struck the path of the robbers on the next morning after their departure, and had encamped each night at the fires which they had left, expecting, as was natural, that they would come to a final stopping place when they had proceeded as far as they liked. Joaquin smiled with exquisite satisfaction when he perceived that Boyce was certainly ahead of him, and from every indication unsuspecting in the remotest degree, that his arch enemy was at that moment in his rear.

At night, after a long day's ride over rugged mountains and deep gulches, Jim Boyce and his company, numbering twenty-five men, including himself, were seated around one of Joaquin's late fires, which they had re-kindled, quietly enjoying their pipes and laughing over the stereotyped jokes which had descended, like Shakespeare, from one generation to another, and are too good ever to be worn out. The heavens were cloudy, and a boundary of solid darkness lay around the lighted ring in which they sat. In the ragged clouds a few stars dimly struggled, and the lonesome scream of the cougar, like the wail of a lost spirit benighted in the infinity of darkness, gave a wild terror to the surrounding woods.

Suddenly and startlingly, the simultaneous reports of fifteen pistols rent the air, the dark outer wall of the fire circle blazed as if a cloud had unbosomed its lightning, and the astonished survivors of the company bounded up to see fifteen of their number stretched upon the earth, and to meet with the deadly repetition of the fifteen revolvers. Panic stricken and bewildered, the survivors of the second discharge, numbering three men, among whom was Jim Boyce, fled headlong into the darkness, and taking no time to choose their ground, hurried madly and distractedly away from the horrible scene.

Joaquin stepped quietly into the circle to see if Jim Boyce was killed, but Three-Fingered Jack leaped in like a demon, with his huge knife in his mutilated hand, which had lost none of its strength, but did its three-fingered work far better than many other whole hands could do it, and soon quenched the last spark of beating life in the pale forms around him. Every one must know that death from a bullet flings a sudden and extreme paleness over the countenance, and thus the light from the fire falling upon the ghastly faces around, displayed a sight so hideous and harrowing, that Joaquin exclaimed with a shudder:

"Let's leave here. We will camp tonight somewhere else."

Searching the bundles upon which the company had been seated, he found in different buckskin purses a sum amounting to not less than thirty thousand dollars. He also added fifteen excellent horses and ten powerful mules to his live stock.

Jim Boyce and his surviving companions wandered to the distant settlements, which, after many hardships, they reached in safety, and it is pleasant to add, that in a short time they raised another company with whom they went back to their rich diggings, and spite of their immense loss by Joaquin's robbery, made for themselves ample fortunes, with which they returned to the Atlantic States. Should Jim Boyce chance to read this humble narrative of mine, I beg him to receive my warmest congratulations.

On one of the head branches of the Mokelumne River, on the last day of December, a large crowd was gathered in and around a cloth building, in a little mining town, which looked like a half venture towards civilization in the midst of that wild and savage region. A tall, dark-skinned man sat in the middle of the room, with a huge log chain around one of his legs. His brow was tall and massive, and his large gray eyes looked forth with that calm, cold light which unmistakably expresses a deep, calculating intellect, divested of all feeling and independent of all motives which arise from mere impulse or passion an intellect which is sole in itself, looking at the result merely in all its actions, not considering the question of right or wrong, and working out a scheme of unmitigated villainy, as it would a mathematical problem.

To the right of this man sat a huge old fellow, with blue eyes, sandy hair, and a severe look, whose scattered law books and papers on the table near by, proclaimed him the Justice of the Peace in that district—an office, by the way, as important at that time in California, and possessing a jurisdiction as extensive as many of the County Courts in other and older States of the Union.

The prisoner was none other than Luis Vulvia, who had been arrested on a charge of murder and robbery in that town on the day before, under the following circumstances:

A German, living by himself in an isolated tent, was heard to scream "murder!" three times; hearing which horrible cry, five or six men some two hundred yards off, ran upto the place, and at a glance comprehended the whole scene. The German lay with his throat cut from ear to ear, and his pockets turned inside-out. Looking hastily around on the outside, they discovered, two men, apparently Mexicans, who dodged on the further side of a deserted cabin and disappeared behind some rocks. Going to the rocks and finding no further trace of the fugitives, they went back and alarmed the whole town with a statement of the circumstances.

Every eye was vigilant in every quarter, and just as Luis Vulvia, who had observed the fast increasing excitement, and guessed pretty nearly the character of its cause, was mounting his horse in front of a liquor saloon, he was suddenly knocked down with a bludgeon, disarmed and securely bound. The people *en masse* securely guarded him during the night which was just at hand, intending to hang him without a trial on the morrow, but were dissuaded by Justice Brown, the tall, severe looking man spoken of, who being a man of influence, and a good speaker withal, convinced them that it was better to proceed with him legally, as there was but little doubt of his being found guilty as one of the murderers, in which case he would deliver him over to their just vengeance. Thus the case stood, up to the moment in which the subject is introduced.

The witnesses, who ran at the cry of murder to the tent, and saw the two Mexicans dodging around the house, could swear no further than that one of them was of about the same size and shape as the prisoner. The barkeeper of the liquor saloon testified in addition to this, that the prisoner rode up to his door and dismounted just before his arrest. It was well known also, that a dozen or more robberies had lately been committed in that neighborhood, and that various persons had met upon the roads a gang of suspicious looking Mexicans armed to the teeth.

This constituted all the testimony against Vulvia, whose person was unknown to the community, but whose name was familiar to all by reputation. Had he been recognized as that noted character, no further inquiry would have been made, but he would have been hurried to the first convenient tree and hung *instanter*. He stood on a dangerous brink. Being asked by the Justice if he had any proof to offer in his own behalf, he replied that he depended upon some of his acquaintances coming in during the day, who would establish his character as an honest man to the satisfaction of the Court.

He affirmed his innocence in a calm tone, and an unflinching manner, although, could his heart have been read, he relied upon the possibility of a rescue by his comrades, which was indeed a feeble hope, looking at the immense crowd who stood scowling upon him from every side. A silence of half an hour rested in the Court, while the Justice was engaged in drawing up a transcript of the case as far as it had proceeded, when a young man superbly dressed, and adorned with a splendid gold watch and chain, entered the room with gentlemanly dignity, and politely addressed the Justice to the following effect.

"My name, your Honor, is Samuel Harrington. I am a merchant and packer in the town of San Jose, and I am just now on my return from the more northern mines, to which I have been packing flour and other provisions. I am encamped within five miles of this place, and having heard from a citizen of your town this morning, that a dark-skinned man, with grey eyes, was in custody on a charge of murder, and that although there was no positive proof against him, yet there was so strong a prejudice against Mexicans, that there was great danger of his being hung by the infuriated populace, it just struck me that the prisoner might be one of my hired men, a Mexican whom I sent into town last night, and who, much to my astonishment, did not return. It is indeed the case. Your prisoner is none other than my packer, and consequently cannot be connected with any robbing or thieving band around here. He has been with me four years, and no man ever sustained a better character. I shall wish, your Honor, to testify in his behalf, but before I take my oath I would like to prove my identity as Mr. Harrington of San Jose. Please examine these letters."

He here presented to the Justice, who was already favorably impressed, five or six letters, addressed in different hands, to "Mr. Samuel Harrington, San Jose," and bearing the marks of various Post Offices in the State. The Justice showed these letters to several of the crowd, whose countenances immediately relaxed towards the prisoner.

"Mr. Harrington," said Squire Brown, "your evidence will be taken without a moment's scruple."

Harrington accordingly testified to the facts which he had already related, and the prisoner was discharged. Many apologies were made to Mr. Harrington for detaining his hired man so long, and after many compliments he and Vulvia departed. As soon as they were clearly out of town, they both indulged in a hearty laugh.

"How came it," said Vulvia to Joaquin, "that you arrived in such good time? I had no expectation but to be hung."

"I happened to reach your camp out here in the mountains last night, having met some of our spies who guided me to it. I had not been there more than two hours before two of your men came in, and reported that they had killed a man in *that little cloth town* and inquired for you. Your being absent immediately created apprehension, and having waited for you anxiously till morning, we were at once convinced that you had been captured. Having most fortunately in my possession a package of letters addressed to Samuel Harrington, San Jose, which I had the good sense to keep, thank God! to preserve at the time I got them into my hands, it immediately flashed on me that in case I found you arrested, I could pass myself off for a respectable merchant, and so save your life. It worked to a charm, as you see. I make it a practice to preserve documents of this kind, and I find that they come in pretty good play."

"But how did you come by them?" inquired Vulvia.

"Oh, easy enough. I killed a fellow on my way down here the other day, and found them in his pockets; and d—d little besides, too."

"You remind me," said Vulvia, "very much of Padre Jurata, God rest his soul! He saved many of his followers by being present at their trials, or introducing witnesses to prove an *alibi*, or presenting forged pardons on the day of execution, signed in the exact hands of the Provincial Governors. His knowledge was extensive, and during his monkish life the confessional had given him so many important and vital secrets connected with great personages, that he could frequently command the services of the wealthiest men and the best born dames of Mexico. Besides this, he sometimes officiated as one of the Fathers in the remote towns and villages."

Thus conversing, they rode on to Vulvia's camp, some ten miles in the mountains, and, were met by a welcome shout from their subordinates.

While at this camp, resting his horses, a messenger arrived from Reis on the Stanislaus, with the news that he had killed one hundred and fifty Chinamen, and had sent to the Arroyo Cantoova two hundred horses since he had last seen his chief.

"Tell him," said Joaquin, "it is all right, and to go ahead; I will send him word before long. Tell him hereafter to send his horses for safe keeping to Quien Sabe Rancho, Rancho Muños, or Joaquin Guerra's Rancho, either of the three."

Reis had managed most cunningly. Hid in an old abandoned tunnel, out of which he had whipped a gang of wolves, he nor any of his party had been seen by daylight at all. All his thefts and robberies had been done in the night. The miserable Chinamen were mostly the sufferers, and they lay along the highways like so many sheep with their throats cut by the wolves. It was a politic stroke in Reis to kill Chinamen in preference to Americans, for no one cared for so alien a class, and they were left to care for themselves.

One moonlight night at the hour of twelve, when silence had fallen upon the world of mountains, woods and valleys, and all quiet spirits were asleep, Reis issued from his tunnel, three hundred feet under ground, with three men, and getting out their horses from the corral of a friendly rancho near by—who was kind enough to take care of them, no doubt from disinterested motives—they started on a pleasure trip up a rather lonesome road, which led along a branch of the South Fork of the Stanislaus River. Coming in sight of a neat looking frame house, Reis, bent upon an adventure, dismounted, as did also his followers, and hitching their horses on the roadside walked stealthily up to the house.

At the first there appeared to be a dead silence about the premises, but going around on the east side, Reis discovered a light burning at a window, and drawing nearer heard the murmuring of voices. Not caring particularly what he did, curiosity led him to look in; which object he readily effected, being a tall man. The sight that met his view was something no less ravishing than a love scene. Upon a settee on the further side of the room, half-reclining, sat a blushing girl of seventeen years, her golden ringlets showered down upon her neck and shoulders, and her bosom heaving as if it would burst its gauzy covering and strike' the gazer blind with its unspeakable loveliness.

At her feet, upon the carpeted floor, knelt a handsome young man, not more than twenty years of age, holding her small white hand in his, which ever and anon he hurried to his lips, and seemed to devour it with kisses. She could not restrain his wild transports, for he caught her with a lover's fierceness around her beautiful neck, and breathed his soul upon her lips. He sprang to her side and pressed her to his bosom as if he would blend his very body with her own. She looked bewildered, the beautiful creature! One moment gently striving to wrest herself from his arms, at another leaning her head upon his bosom with a sigh of unutterable love.

It was a sight which might well disturb the equanimity of any man, and it is not to be wondered at that Reis looked on like one bewitched. Fate at last had some mercy on the bandit for after he had swallowed his uprising heart a hundred times with looking on the enchanted beauty of the passionate girl in her lover's arms, the latter tore-himself away and started forth from the house. One of the bandits followed him as a matter of course, while Reis hastily concerted with the others how to act—for he was determined to abduct the girl at all hazards.

The young man was walking very leisurely along in a bend of the road, when he heard a sharp click just behind him. With sudden surprise he looked around, and there, face to face with him stood a man, or devil, or whatever else it might be, with a cocked pistol pointed within six inches of his head.

"Down on your knees, or I will blow your brains out."

The young man knelt now from a different motive to that which made him kneel a short time before.

"Shell out you dastardly scoundrel!" said the accomplished highwayman.

"There, take it," and threw his purse a few feet from him on the ground.

The robber stooped to pick it up, and while he was bent the young man drew a small dagger from his bootleg and plunged it into his back. It struck him directly in the spine, and the huge-bodied villain sunk without a groan.

The young man, vaguely suspecting that there might be danger lurking near his Rosalie, went back to the house. To his horror, his ears were saluted with a loud and piercing scream. Like a madman he rushed to the house, and had just entered the door of Rosalie's room, and taken one glance, which showed him the terrified girl struggling in the hands of a savage-looking monster, when he was knocked senseless to the floor. The gray-haired old mother, a lonely widow, whose only pleasure was her daughter, clung to the robber's arm, and in the trembling accents of extreme old age, beseeched him—while the tears flooded the wrinkled channels of her face—to spare her child, her only child.

"Cease your gabbling," said one of Reis' men, who knocked the old lady speechless at his feet.

"Who told you to do that?" said Reis, and instantly shot the officious scoundrel through the heart.

"Now my pretty duck you can come along with me," he said turning to his captive.

But at the sight of the ruffian's blow, which felled her mother, Rosalie's blue eyes had closed in a swoon, and paleness as of death had overspread her features.

"It makes no difference," said Reis to his surviving companion, "she will soon get over it anyhow; let us go along."

"I don't know that I care about going just now," the cut-throat replied, looking black as a thunder cloud, "after what you have done to poor Francisco there," laying his hand on his pistol at the same time.

"You don't, eh?" said Reis, "then you are as trifling a scoundrel as he is."

The two fired at once; the subordinate fell dead, and Reis was grazed on his right cheek with a piece of hot lead, which made him blush, if his own villainy did not.

"Blast the two miserable scoundrels," said he "it actually seems as if some men had no humanity at all."

Tying the rounded wrists of his lovely drooping captive with his handkerchief, he proceeded to the spot where the horses were hitched, cut them loose, all but his own, and mounted into his saddle with his precious booty before him. The loosened horses dashed back to the corral from which they had been taken, and Reis rode on by himself, till within a quarter of a mile of his tunnel, when he got down with his now weeping burden, turned his horse loose, which followed after the others, and proceeded on foot at his leisure.

Rosalie begged him to release her, with so much sorrowful sweetness in her voice, with so beautiful an agony expressive in her whole enchanting form, that the rocky-hearted Reis almost repented of what he had done.

"It won't do," he thought, "to let her go now, for I will have nothing to show for my night's work, and how should I account to the band for the missing members?"

"You sha'nt be hurt," said he, turning mildly towards the trembling maiden, "I am going to keep you only a few days, until I can get a ransom for you, which some of your friends will no doubt pay, when you send them word by one of our number."

They soon reached the entrance of the tunnel, into which he dragged the shuddering girl, and led her, half dead with terror, into the extreme end, where sat his fierce-looking companions in a well lighted apartment.

The bandits, much interested, gathered around their captain, who informed them—"that he had attacked a certain house on the road and succeeded in entering, but found no money, which disappointed him so much that he took this beautiful girl in the place of it;" and further stated, "that in the struggle at the house, two of his men were killed before his face, and one was missing, he being probably killed, as well as the others. As for this handsome girl," he concluded, "we may as well keep her for a ransom, or one of us may marry her, just as we, see fit."

Poor, poor Rosalie! May Heaven protect you, for man cannot.

Rosalie on the second night after her capture, resolved to help herself. Rising from a warm couch of blankets already dressed, and unperceived by the bandits, who lay slumbering around, she started into the throat of the tunnel in order to find her way out. Pressing her hand to her heart to still its loud beatings, she stepped noiselessly along, until she had left the sleeping apartment, when looking forward, she saw that every light in front of her had been extinguished.

Pausing with indefinable dread at the thought of walking that fearful passage alone, she heard a loud yawn from one of the sleepers, as if he were waking, and with a sudden movement, which was scarce voluntary, she shot like an arrow into the blackness which lay before her. On and on, and on she moved with trembling footsteps, feeling her way on the sides of the tunnel, and placing her feet each time with the indescribable terrible feeling that she might be stepping off into some deep abyss below. It seemed ages to her, before she could reach the entrance. Oh, that she might but catch one friendly glimpse of light!

It appears—a faint, flickering gleam in the distance. With hurrying feet she approaches,—larger and larger it grows, until she sees the lamp, like a full-blown rose of light swinging from the arch; joy! Her escape is certain. She stands now in the fall blaze, she sees no one, and with a more confident heart pursues her way. She was now near the entrance. She saw the moonlight flooding the world without, and rushed eagerly forward. A huge figure started suddenly before her, and the beautiful girl fainted. It was a bad time to swoon, but how could so delicate an organization, fit only to be played upon by the subtlest flashes of thought, sporting in rainbow-fancies, sustain so rude a shock? She fell gasping for breath, and the sentinel, for it was he, carried her to the apartment which she had left, and tenderly laid her upon her couch, without disturbing any one in the room, and hurried back to his post.

So tenderly delicate was this innocent creature, so divine the appealing spirit of her eyes as he looked into her face, that Reis could not find it in his heart to treat her with anything but the profoundest respect. He had seized her in a moment of passion, stung with her voluptuous beauty, and would at that moment have fought for her, as for a conquest of so much of Heaven itself. Such is the maddening effect of beauty upon the hearts of men! But on sober reflection he banished the vain idea, which he had been foolish enough to vaguely entertain, that she could ever love a man like him, rude and uncouth as he was, and seriously contemplated restoring her to her aged and widowed mother, and one whom he knew that she loved.

Confused and tormented with doubt, she was a continual trouble on his hands. He was not scoundrel enough to force her into a vile position, and he was afraid to leave her for a moment in the hands of his less scrupulous comrades. Already had they began to murmur at him for his weakness, and he had been forced to threaten some of their lives, if they did not keep their distance from the girl. There was danger of a mutiny, and so critical was his situation, that notwithstanding he dreaded Joaquin's opinion of his conduct in this specific matter, yet he longed to see him.

Reis was sitting one night, moping in his-tunnel like a grim wolf, and scowling discontentedly around him, for he had done nothing for a week, when the sentinel came in attended by two persons, whom he left standing before Reis, and returned to his post. The melancholy bandit raised his head, and beheld his now dreaded chief before him. Joaquin glanced hastily around the room and beholding the captive-girl reclining mournfully upon her couch, he started, and with a sudden fierceness, which made every man in his presence quail, turned to Reis, and said with a look that rived his soul:

"How is this? Did I ever instruct you to engage in a business of this kind? Explain yourself, or by G—d, it will not be well for you."

Reis begged, him to listen patiently, and related every circumstance connected with the girl's capture, his killing his two comrades at the time, and everything which followed subsequently.

Joaquin was in a tempest of anger.

"So you have done nothing but mope for the past week,—essential service you have rendered to our organization. Reis," he continued, convulsively clutching his pistol handle, "if it was any other man but you, I would kill him on the spot. I would shoot him like a dog. But d—n you," he exclaimed with sudden vehemence, while his eyes blazed as none but his could, "have you done her any injury? Have you taken any advantage of that girl, sir?"

"No, no. You know that I would scorn to do that," replied Reis.

"I believe you, and it is well that it is so Reis," he continued in a calmer tone, "I am surprised at you. I have never done a thing of this kind. I have higher purposes in view than to torture innocent females. I would have no woman's person without her own consent. I have read of robbers who deliberately ravished tender and delicate females, and afterwards cut their throats, but I despise them. I am no such robber, and I never will be. Reis, I ought to kill you, but since you have had *some* honor and manhood about you in this rascally matter, I will let you off this time. Get you in readiness, and we will, you and I alone, return this girl to her mother, if the poor old woman be alive, and forth with set this matter right. I wouldn't at such a time as this, be bothered by a frivolous matter of this kind, for all the women in the world, spread out in a perfect sea of bosoms and lips!"

Rosalie, who had been listening with intense interest to every word, at this moment sprang towards the young chief, whose appearance was far from forbidding, even to the most refined female, and in a fit of uncontrollable gratitude and rapture, at the prospect of her deliverance, threw her arms around his neck before she thought. Recovering herself instantly, she thanked him in a dignified manner for his noble conduct, and told him that she respected him from the bottom of her heart, robber as he was.

Joaquin looked at her proudly, as he laid his hand upon his breast, and said:

"Yes, Senorita, I *am* a man. I was once as noble a man as ever breathed, and if I am not so now, it is because men would not allow me to be as I wished. You shall return to your mother and to your lover, if I die in bringing it about."

On this same night at eleven o'clock stood the frame house on the road that leads up on a branch of the South Fork of the Stanislaus River, the same as it was on that happy, sorrowful night, when Rosalie was embraced by her lover, and torn from his presence. In one of the rooms sat her old disconsolate mother, whose withering life was alone sustained by the hope of seeing her daughter again, and near her the young man Edward—. He was comforting the old lady with assurances, which did not quiet his own heart, for he had ridden day and night over one-half of the county, making inquiries in every quarter, but not a trace could he find of the missing girl or her abductor.

His face was pale and thin with anxiety, and his voice had something hollow in it, as though the vampire of despair was sucking his heart's blood. He began to believe that his adored Rosalie was lost to him forever, and was doomed to a fate he could not contemplate without a shuddering chill. After soothing the feeble brain of the old woman with what he knew to be the merest illusions, he had subsided into silence, and was eating his heart in bitter regret, when a sudden tap was heard on the door and in a moment leaped into the room the very object of his thoughts. The meeting was such as might be expected. But I will not fill this sheet with an attempt at a description of it.

Edward's rapture, astonishment, bewilderment of joy!—The old decrepid mother's scarce audible syllables, and her far more expressive tears. Rapidly was her story recounted by Rosalie, and with such enthusiasm did she dwell on the heroic conduct of Joaquin, that her lover almost became jealous of the young robber. She made him swear that he would never injure *that man*, whatever he might do to others.

"I won't touch Joaquin," he replied, "if he lets me alone, but as for that other bloody beast. I will kill him the first time I lay my eyes on him."

Joaquin at this moment walked in, and stood before the young man. Reis very prudently remained on the outside, after hearing the observation which had just been made respecting him.

"I have done you a favor, sir," said Joaquin, "and now I want you to keep this matter a profound secret. Never breathe my name out of this house. I will be in this county for some time, but you and yours shall not be troubled. But if you betray me, I will scatter to the winds all that you have, and all that you love."

"It is hard," said the young man, "to be under obligations to a man like you, but I will be silent."

"And who are *you*, pray, that talk as if it were stooping to be under obligations to a man like me?" and the fiery spirit of Joaquin leaped into his eyes. He touched the hilt of his bowie-knife when a supplicating look from Rosalie checked him.

Edward—drew his revolver half out, but Rosalie touched his arm; and with a reproachful look, said to him—

"Fie, fie, Edward, you forget yourself. You wouldn't harm the man who has restored me to your arms? Why, Edward, would you make me despise you? I care not if he were a robber a thousand times, he is a noble man; shake hands with him," and taking his hand with her left, and the robber's with her right, she joined them together with a gentle force.

Sternly the young men looked at each other for a second, and then, with a half-friendly, half-defiant smile, they parted.

Joaquin and Reis rode off, the one somewhat reconciled to his subordinate, since the issue had been good, and the other delighted beyond all bounds at the happy turn which things had taken.

"I would have given her up long ago," exclaimed Reis, "but my men would have killed me for it, I am certain. It was fortunate that you came when you did, or the poor girl would have been far worse off than she is now, the beautiful creature that she is!" said he, with enthusiasm.

Rosalie and Edward—, were shortly after married. They kept their secret while Joaquin lived, and for my part, I do not blame them.

XI

Terrible Scenes in Calaveras County—More Harboring Places for the Robbers Named—Desperate Conflict of Deputy Sheriff Ellas with Joaquin and Eight of His Men

The new year opened—the ever memorable year of 1853—and by the middle of January the bold and accomplished bandit was ready to enter upon a series of the bloodiest scenes that ever were enacted in the same space of time, in any age or country. Calaveras county, as I have said before, the richest, or among the richest, at least, in the Golden State, he chose as the theatre of his operations, and never was a region so scourged and desolated. Detached parties numbering four, five or a dozen men were scattered over the face of the whole country, and so diverse were their operations, so numerous and swift that I shall not attempt to give a minute account of all of them, but shall confine myself particularly to the individual movements of Joaquin, and strictly to those facts which are absolutely known, and traceable to their original source.

It may be distinctly set down, however, in the outset, that though many villainous deeds which transpired in the short period which I am about to make a sketch of, were mysterious and unaccountable; many murders committed in parts remote from each other, robberies here, thefts there, and destruction, lightning-footed, treading everywhere, invisible in its approach, and revealed only in the death trail which it left behind, yet all this mighty and seemingly chaotic scene had its. birth in the dramatic brain of Joaquin—an author who acted out his own tragedies! Divergent as were the innumerable lines of action, yet they were all concentrated, morally, upon one point, and directed to one purpose, that which existed in the breast of Joaquin.

There was not a town of any importance in that whole region in which he had not a spy, one or more, located; not one in which he had hot his agents and secret friends. He lacked not for harboring places in which to conceal his wounded men and stolen animals. Numerous ranchos, owned by "wealthy and respectable men," as the world goes, have been mentioned to me as places which afforded him refuge and assistance whenever needed. Among the number which were named with particular emphasis, were the Los Alamos Rancho, on the Rio

Napoma, the Ortego Rancho and the Concho Rancho. Some of the suspected ranchos, it is but justice to say, have since changed hands.

Around San Andreas, Caliveritas and Yackee Camp, numerous thefts and robberies had been committed in the space of a few weeks. Property was missed, but no one knew whither it was gone. Men were murdered, and the bloody hand remained unseen. Yet everyone knew that thieves and murderers walked unknown in the midst of the community. The strange dread hung over every face, and gave vigilance to every eye. The fearful shrunk back from a danger which they could *feel*, but not see. The bold stood forward with their lives in their hands, to search into, find and face the perils which existed around them, the more terrible that they were disguised and concealed.

Among the boldest, most firm and energetic, whom the crisis brought forth, was Captain Charles H. Ellas, of San Andreas, who in his capacity as Deputy Sheriff of Calaveras county, took the lead in ferreting out the perpetrators of these foul deeds. He was a young man of fine appearance, slenderly formed, but making up for the want of superior strength in great activity and astonishing powers of endurance. His eyes were keen, quick and flashing, touched with a fierceness which at times seemed to scorch where it fell. A chivalrous son of the South; he had grown up under a discipline which taught him that honor was a thing to be maintained at the sacrifice of blood, or of life itself; that fear was a feeling too base to harbor in a manly breast, aid that *he* was a coward who would not give the question of his rights to the arbitration of steel or of the deadly ball. Already did his bosom bear the marks of severe and dangerous hand-to-hand conflicts, a trial of muscle, nerve and skill, in a game whose stake is human life, and whose hazard is eternity.

At a juncture so important as the period of which I speak, a man like Elias was most naturally looked to as a leader, and entrusted with a large amount of discretionary power, so necessary to be used in perilous times, when the slow forms of law, with their snail-like processes, are altogether useless and inefficient.

The first opportunity which presented itself for anything like determinate action, occurred about the middle of January. Some horses were stolen at the town of San Andreas, and a description of the Mexicans who took them had been given to Captain Ellas, who in the course of a day's ride on the various roads, accidentally discovered the party on the road leading from Yackee Camp to Chaparral Hill.

They had added two to their number, who were not perceived, however, by the Captain at the first glance. Seeing two mounted men on a small hill to the left of the road, he hailed them, and requested them to come down as he had something to say. One of them replied:

"If you want to see us more than we do you, come to us."

Whereupon Ellas advanced, but the intermediate space being marshy, much rain having lately fallen, his horse mired so bad that he dismounted. Proceeding on foot, he heard a rustling in the brush to the right, which sounded very much, like an ambush, ready to burst forth, but he kept on his way. When within eighty yards of the two to whom he had spoken, he saw that they had drawn their revolvers. This hostile movement, and the rustling in the brush to the right, convinced him that he was acting a very imprudent part, and that he was even then in very imminent danger. With much presence of mind he looked behind him, and gave a signal-whistle, as if he had a company in waiting, which stratagem succeeded so well that the two in open sight rode slowly over the hill, and those who had been concealed precipitately left the thicket.

Going to where his horse was feeding, he mounted and rode over to Yackee Camp, a little mining town a few miles distant, in order to get men to go out with him in further pursuit. He found no one at all prepared to accompany him, but a Mexican merchant in the place, named Atanacio Moreno, a man who was worth money, and stood well in the community. Unsuspected by Ellas, this man secretly belonged to the band of Joaquín Murieta, or, I should rather say, to the tremendous organization which that bold chieftain had established throughout the country. The Captain had unlimited confidence in this individual, for he had previously assisted him in the capture of a horse thief, and besides giving him much valuable information, had furnished men and horses in various expeditions started by the honest portion of the community.

He was treacherous, and though assisting to capture individuals sometimes who belonged to his own fraternity, they were always those whom he hated personally. A dangerous companion in a lonely ride! Moreno, pretending to have watched through his spies the movements of the depredators, led the way over the mountains, valleys, and gulches until sunset, but no trace of the objects sought was found, and the pursuit was here relinquished.

It became known before a great while, for a certainty, that this man was a scoundrel, and leaving the country in a few weeks after his connection with Joaquin was discovered, he joined *Senati*, a petty robber of some note in the south. He had not been with that leader long, before he secretly assassinated him, cut off his head, and delivered it to the civil authorities of the town of Los Angeles for' a reward of five hundred dollars, which had been offered for it. This act of treachery did not avail him much, for he was afterwards arrested on a grave charge, and thrown into prison, and afterwards hung.

XII

Attack of Joaquin Upon Americans in Yackee Camp—Joaquin Empties His Six-Shooter, and Throws His Sword in the Fight—Capture of Joaquin's Friend, the Gambler Bill, and His Summary Execution—Harboring Places and Dens of the Robbers Mobbed and Burned

It was soon ascertained, that an organized band of robbers was in the community of San Andreas and vicinity. Yackee Camp was discovered to be their rendezvous, situated about two miles and a half from San Andreas. Upon this discovery, Captain Ellas employed a number of spies to gather all the information that they could in relation to the thieves and robbers, whose leader was not then known. While these spies were out, Captain Ellas one day rode into Yackee Camp, and was seated on his horse near a little drinking house, observing matters and things in that very suspicious vicinity, when, he perceived a young, black-eyed, fine looking fellow, standing with his cloak wrapped around him, very intently fixing his gaze upon himself, the Captain.

As soon as their eyes met, the young fellow drew the rim of his hat over his face, and flinging his cloak a little back from his shoulder, dropped his arm down carelessly toward the butt of his pistol. In a moment more he turned and walked off. Captain Ellas will no doubt recollect the circumstance, and must not be surprised to learn that this was none other than Joaquin, himself, who thus took his daguerreotype upon memory, and found it afterwards of much avail in aiding him to escape danger, and to keep out of the way when he saw the original at the head of an armed party, or otherwise to direct his movements to the best advantage. The Captain did not at this time even know Joaquin was in the county, although the renowned robber's name was familiar to his ears, by the report of his depredations in other counties for a long time back.

The spies, after the lapse of several days, returned with the information that they had discovered several lurking places of the robbers, among which was Chaparral Hill, a description of which it may be as well to give, inasmuch as it was the scene of quite an interesting event. It lies to the southwest of San Andreas about four miles, and is nothing more than an elevated pass between two steep ridges, which are crowned with precipitous rocks, whose interstices would effectually conceal a man from observation. Thickets of chaparral cover various spots on the tops of the ridges, with open spaces between, and in many places the liveoak trees with low branches, and crooked knotty trunks, form, a kind of natural fortification, almost as perfect as if they had been arranged expressly for the purpose. The pass itself is but a lowering of a long curving wall (a natural wall) which connects the two ridges together, and between these ridges a long hollow leads up, and terminates at the pass.

By the foot of the hollow run a clear little stream, margined with green grass, called Willow Creek, because it is infringed so beautifully with the lithe and graceful trees of that name. Behind the curving wall described, a steep descent goes down to the valley below, and is covered with immense grease-wood thickets, taller than a man's head, through which a party pursued could make a safe retreat, and through which it would be dangerous to follow them.

A few tall pines stand isolated here and there, on the different eminences, which shoot up in rugged majesty from the general outline. One ridge terminates at the connecting wall, but the other stretches on a mile or two beyond it, marked by a bridle trail, which suddenly plunges into a succession of deep ravines and gulches, lined with greasewood and low timber—lonely and sombre looking places From this pass, or any place adjacent, a view of the country is commanded many miles in extent.

A few days after the return of the spies, a gentleman by the name of Hall, who kept a rancho on the road leading from Mokelumne Hill to San Andreas, called on Ellas and informed him that three Mexicans had passed his house that morning, who looked suspicious, they having but two horses, and one of the men in consequence mounted behind another. One of these men had been detained by him at his house, having stopped but a few moments while the others rode on, but remained no longer than he saw fit after all, for upon the first movements towards preventing his free agency, he drew a revolver and walked out. Hall and a man named Davis followed the party about a mile, and saw where they had left the main road, and gone up Murray's Creek.

Ellas mounted his horse, accompanied by his friend, a young lawyer of fine parts, by the name of Wm. J. Gatewood, who had practiced at squirrels and turkeys in the woods as much as he had practiced at the bar, and was as skillful in drawing a "bead" as in drawing a brief—

and attended also by Hall, Davis and another man whose name is not remembered—Hall being provided with a pistol, Davis with a rifle, and the other man with a yager. The party numbered five, hastily gotten up, and but poorly prepared for a combat; but supposing he was only on the track of three Mexicans, the Captain proceeded on their trail.

Immediately after starting he met a gentleman named Peter Woodbeck, whom, having a little business with, he requested to ride back a short distance with the company.

Arriving at Murray's Creek he struck a fresh trail of two horses, as expected, about a mile from San Andreas, leading behind a ridge of mountains that skirted that little town showing that the riders had kept themselves concealed from view of the main road, until immediately opposite San Andreas, at which point they had evidently ridden to the top of the ridge, and who no doubt saw their pursuers start out, and at the same time counted their number. The trail from this point led over the mountains towards Yackee Camp, which gave Ellas to suppose they were a part of the band said to be lurking about Chaparral Hill. He immediately sent Peter Woodbeck to San Andreas with a request to Alcalde Taliaferro to send two parties of men, each numbering five, and have them stationed on the different trails leading from the Chaparral Hill.

The Alcalde being ill, was unable to attend personally to the request, but used every exertion in his power by his agents, to raise the two parties needed, unfortunately without success. Under the impression that the men would be stationed as desired, the Captain rode on. The trail wound along in a very circuitous manner over the roughest possible places, so that it was in the afternoon before he reached the foot of the hollow before spoken of, at Willow Creek, only four miles from San Andreas. Ascending the hollow, the pursuing party immediately saw on the curve of the pass of Chaparral Hill, several Mexicans mounted upon fine horses, and rode up towards them until within rifle shot, when they halted.

Two or three of the Mexicans rode down behind some bushes and rocks on the slant, and commenced firing at them with Colt's heavy pistols, but without effect. Ellas and party immediately shifted their position to a place within fair pistol shot, during which movement Davis levelled his rifle at a fellow partially hid in the rocks, and evidently hit him. The man with the yager in vain tried to fire it—it would not "go off," and the weapon remained useless through the whole fight, as well as the bearer of it, who had nothing else with which to do battle.

Though sadly needed he stood neutral, ap far as any service he could do was concerned, but served admirably well as a target for the bandits to practice at, nevertheless.

To aggravate the state of things, Davis, after discharging his rifle, could find no more bullets in his pouch, and was thus also rendered unable to do anything. Only three men therefore were left to do the fighting! The Mexicans noticing this dilemma, dashed along on the curve of the hill, nine in number, splendidly mounted and well armed—some were observed to have two revolvers each. While passing they fired about twenty shots, but were riding so rapidly that they could not shoot with much precision.

As it was, Gatewood's mule was severely wounded in the neck, and bled profusely. A ball passed across Ellas' breast, burning a hole in the side of his vest, and another went through his hair. After this swoop of theirs they retired to their first position. A portion of them then dismounting, crept down behind the bushes, so as to get near enough to Ellas' party to make a dead shot, and commenced firing, but not with the desired certainty, for Ellas and Gatewood had dismounted, and were somewhat protected by their animals. The Captain finding an opportunity for the first time to fire with any chance of hitting, shot at a large Mexican who stood on the edge of a bush, who suddenly retired to the top of the hill.

Upon the report of his pistol, his mare, a fine, well trained animal, went down the hollow about four hundred yards towards Willow Creek, when one of the mounted Mexicans dashed around as if to secure her.

She ran back towards Ellas, and the Mexican followed to within seventy yards, immediately below him. Ellas fired, and the fellow sunk on the neck of his horse, apparently badly wounded. Four or five of the Mexicans noticing this, galloped along the ridge towards the side of the hill to which the wounded Mexican had retired, and effectually covered his position, so that it was impossible to approach him without receiving their fire. He was then wrapping his red scarf around his breast, as if endeavoring to stop the blood. Ellas' horse soon dashed to the left of the Mexicans, and came up to him, when he mounted and led his party around towards the right hand ridge, in order to gain the summit, if possible, which object he hoped to effect while the opposing force was somewhat separated.

In passing under a steep rocky place, Gatewood exclaimed, "There is a Mexican above us!" and had scarcely finished the sentence before the fellow commenced firing with his revolver. He fired three distinct shots at a distance of not more than forty yards. Ellas suddenly wheeling his horse, discovered him almost perpendicularly over his head not more than thirty yards distant, mounted upon a white horse; and taking a steady aim with his six-shooter, pulled the trigger. The Mexican fell back upon his saddle, wounded in the breast, but soon recovering himself put spurs to his horse and darted out of sight.

Up to this time the Captain had concluded to risk this very disadvantageous battle, in the hope that the two parties sent by Peter Woodbeck would arrive on the two trails in the rear of the robbers; but finding that they were not likely to come, and knowing that he was exposing himself and his comrades to be shot down in detail from behind the rocks and bushes, he decided to retire to the' foot of the hollow, where his opponents could not assail him without exposure to, themselves. They did not follow him, and after a short consultation with his comrades, he started back for San Andreas, which he reached without difficulty, and immediately proceeded to organize a party.

While doing this, word came from Yackee Camp that six men, evidently of the same band, had come down into that place from the direction of Chaparral Hill, and without a moment's parley, had commenced killing the few Americans with whom they happened to meet Joaquin (for it was with him that Ellas had been fighting without knowing it) rode among the houses during the shooting, and remarked:

"This is not my fight; this is Bill's fight," alluding to an affray between one of his friends, named Bill, who was a Mexican gambler in the place, and some Americans, which had occurred a short time before.

When this remark was made Three-Fingered Jack discharged his pistol at an American who was standing near, and killed him on the spot. Another American whom Joaquin recognized, started to run; he was on foot, but ran with as much speed over the rough ground, which had been dug up and ditched in various places by the miners, as did the robber chief, who pursued him on horseback. Leaping and plunging through the holes and ditches, Joaquin shot at him six times without effect, and having thus emptied his six-shooter, finally threw at him his two edged sword, which barely missed the poor fellow's neck just as he escaped in a ledge of rocks.

It was a trying scene for any one to pass through, and of a character such as he would not soon forget. Joaquin reloaded his revolver, recovered his sword, and rode back into town, swearing that he would get even on that day's work if it took him twenty years, for he had lost three of his best men on Chaparral Hill.

"G-d d-n that little Sheriff of San Andreas," said he, "I knew him all the time!"

Soon after, having cleared out the Americans in Yackee Camp, he galloped off with his men, numbering six, over the hills towards the mountains, leaving one wounded horse, which had been shot at the late skirmish at the pass.

Upon receiving this information, Ellas started for Yackee Camp with his party, consisting of six mounted men, followed by some thirty citizens of San Andreas, on foot. Arriving at the tragical scene, they immediately seized the Mexican gambler Bill, who had been foolish enough to remain after Joaquin's remark about him, and having subjected him to a California trial, they sentenced him to be hung "forthwith," as a member of Joaquin's band. He begged them earnestly to spare his life, but finding it was in vain, his brow darkened, and with an air of proud defiance he told them to do their work.

"By going to my trunk," said he, "you will find a knife, from whose blade no handkerchief has yet wiped the d-d American blood."

This speech did not serve to mollify the state of feeling toward him, and he was jerked up into a tree, and strangled with very little ceremony.

It was now a late hour in the night, but there remained a finishing stroke to be put upon the proceedings before retiring to rest. The harboring places and dens of the robbers were found out, and the enraged citizens went to work tearing down and burning up the houses of this character. The conflagration lit up the vault of heaven, and its sound roared among the mountains for miles around.

Around the smouldering ruins, guards and pickets were stationed till morning, and the wearied citizens slept.

XIII

Three Companies of Americans Or Ganized—Pursuit of Robbers—Desperate Conflict at the Phoenix Quartz Mill—One of the Robbers Wounded and Taken Prisoner—His Harborer Shot and Killed—A Mexican Hung For Confession—He Confesses—A Spy Captured—He Falls Into the Hands of Cherokees—Murders and Hanging—Digger Indian and "Paper Talk"—Bad Judgement of Two Americans and a German—Chinamen Suffer—Three-Fingered Jack Has Two Tremendous Races On Horseback—More Hanging—Slaughter of Chinamen—Combat Between Prescott and Joaquin

At daylight three companies were organized, two mounted and one on foot, whose object was to break up the whole confederacy of robbers and their harborers, and never to rest until the neighborhood should be free from them. A man named Henry Scroble took charge of one mounted company, and Ellas of the other. The former proceeded over the mountains, and Ellas over the lower hills in a different direction. It was sometime before the companies could be fairly started, and meanwhile Joaquin, accompanied by the five men who were left to him after the fight at Chaparral Hill, and who had seen the burning of his friends' houses at Yackee Camp, had I come down full of vengeance, as far as the Phoenix Quartz Mill, a few miles from Yackee Camp, and there had met two Americans whom he had immediately attacked.

One of them was Peter Woodbeck, who was known by the robbers, having been marked by them when on the day before Ellas had sent him back', with word to Alcalde Taliaferro. He was just mounting his horse at the quartz mill, when Joaquin rode up.

"You are my meat," said Joaquin, and drew his revolver.

Woodbeck replied, "We will see," and drew his.

Three-Fingered Jack rode towards Woodbeck's companion, who, being on foot, fired one shot from a derringer pistol and dashed into the mill. Three-Fingered Jack, after emptying two loads at him as he fled, which perforated the building near the door, dismounted and rushed, with bowie knife in hand after him.

There a desperate hand to hand conflict ensued, the American defending himself with a short bar of iron. But Three-Fingered Jack triumphed, and his bowie knife drank the poor fellow's heart's blood. He came dragging him out by the hair of the head, and the fight between Woodbeck and Joaquin was still going on, the relative positions of the two not allowing any chance for Joaquin's friends to assist him. Woodbeck being wounded, and having emptied his revolver at his antagonist without effect, now put spurs to his horse to fly the field, and was nearly out of pistol range when Three-Fingered Jack fired at the horse and struck him so centre a shot that he fell dead in his tracks. The bloody monster then rushed up and "finished" the unfortunate rider upon the spot.

The bodies of these men were yet warm when Ellas and his company rode up, and stood horrified at the bloody spectacle.

The trail of the murderers from the Quartz Mill was plain, leading over the San Domingo Creek range of mountains, following which Ellas and company met with the foot company, which had been detailed to go through the rougher part of the mountainous section near the Cherokee Flat. They gave him some interesting information, which was, that they had found clothing which had evidently been thrown from a wounded man, and upon the discovery had proceeded immediately to a camp not far off, where they found two Mexicans, one of them badly wounded. The sound one rose to his feet, and started at full speed, but was shot, so that he died in a short time afterwards in an adjacent thicket to which he ran before he fell. This individual was not a "fighting member," but rather a sly and secret friend, who had volunteered to take care of one of Joaquin's wounded men, who had been hit in the skirmish at Chaparral Hill the day before.

They also saw in a neighboring thicket of chaparral three other mounted men of the robber band, whom they did not find an opportunity to attack. The wounded man was still lying at the camp, unable to get out of the way without help. It was dark when Ellas received this information, but determined to lose no opportunity of meeting with the scoundrels, he stationed men around the chaparral thickets to watch during the night, sent others to arrest the wounded robber at the camp, and to convey him to Cherokee Flat, and hurried off two others to two different ferries on the Stanislaus River, with orders to the ferrymen to allow no one to cross. The wounded man being a trouble upon their hands, and no doubt being entertained as to his character, the Cherokee half-breeds, and others at the Cherokee House, concluded to hang him, a very necessary ceremony, which was soon performed.

Ellas lay watching the camp from which the wounded robber had been taken, all night, in the hope that some of his companions might come; but none arrived. Early in the morning he gathered his party and started on a bush trail over the Bear Mountain, scaling its highest point. In several places along this trail he found spots where men had manifestly stopped, and thrown up clotted blood from their stomachs. Tracking on he reached a Chinese Camp, which the Chinamen informed them had just been robbed by three Mexicans, who took their last dime, and barely allowed them to escape with their lives.

Hurrying forward from here, he found that they had crossed the river at Forman's Rancho, despite all efforts to prevent them. Upon the other side they struck the main road which led along its banks, and their distinct trail was lost among the number of tracks common to a public highway. On the next day, still indefatigably searching through the woods He again found their trail which conducted him within a mile of San Andreas, and was again lost in the main road. All trace of them was then lost for three or four days, at the expiration of which, as the Captain was riding along with three followers, a friendly Mexican named Jesus Ahoa came up to him, and informed him that he had noticed some Mexicans leading horses over a mountain near Greaserville on the Calaveras River, who looked exceedingly suspicious.

Following Jesus Ahoa as a guide, Ellas and his three comrades rode to the mountain indicated, and very readily fell upon the trail. Proceeding a few miles' they found three horses which had been lariated on the way in a sequestered spot, between two steep ridges.

Further on they found two or three Americans, who had seen Joaquin and two others pass them not a great while before, riding at full speed down the river, Joaquin being mounted on a thoroughbred mare. Ellas, with his usual energy diligently pursued their trail until the dusk of the evening, when he arrived, at an isolated drinking house, whose inmates refused to give any information whatever concerning the pursued party. The trail was yet visible, and led down to the bank of the Calaveras River, which he crossed, finding the trail without much difficulty. It ran up-the river a short distance, and recrossed it.

The Captain did the same, and found it again upon the first bank. It led out a short distance towards Angel's Camp, a little mining town a few miles off, but doubled upon itself again, and again crossed the river.

It was now dark, and impossible to find the lost trail, even if it had been practicable to follow it when found. The pursuit was accordingly given up for that night. The next morning the Captain rode up to an isolated house in a wild section of the mountains, where lived a rough looking Mexican, solitary and alone, and discovered at his door the tracks of several horses, which he knew were the same horses that had made the trail of the day before, from the peculiarity in one of the hoofs, which was very distinctly impressed at every step.

The ill-looking fellow denied all knowledge of any mounted men having been to his house. A lariat was speedily attached to his neck, and he was sent up into a tree to see if he could not obtain the desired information. Having been sent up twice, he ascertained the important fact that Joaquin had passed his house the night before with two other men, and had told him that he was going to Campo Seco, on his way to the city of Marysville in the northern country—that the neighborhood was getting too warm for him, and he wanted a little fresh air; that he intended to return, for he would never rest satisfied until he had the heart's blood of Ellas and the Mexican who had put the Captain on his trail, etc.

THE NEXT DAY AFTER THIS the Captain ascertained that Joaquin had crossed the Stanislaus River at Lancha Plana with his party, forcing the ferryman to act contrary to orders, and put him over. He had scarcely landed on the other side when he was attacked by Americans, for it must be borne in mind that the whole country was aroused, who being Superior in number, poured hot lead into his midst with such bewildering rapidity that he was compelled to fly with the utmost precipitation, leaving in his hurry several very fine loose horses. It was supposed that he soon afterward swam the river at another place, and was still in the neighborhood. Accompanied by a gentleman from Angel's Camp, Ellas went to the fastnesses of the Bear Mountain range, in the hope to discover fresh trails; found one which led towards a camp called Los Muertos; the tracks indicating that there were five mounted men.

Being in no condition to follow them, he rode over to Cherokee Flat, and requested a number of Cherokees, located there, to go out and way-lay the different trails between Bear Mountain and San Domingo Range, to which they readily assented. In the meantime a meeting of the citizens was held at Carson's Creek, to take measures in the pressing exigency, which was upon that district, in common with others.

A Mexican was noticed in the meeting attentively noticing its proceedings, who as soon as it was broken up, was seen to go to a bakery, purchase a quantity of bread, and start off on foot toward Bear Mountain. He was followed and seized on the side of the mountain, and at the same time his captors discovered three Mexicans riding on the ridge a few hundred yards above them. One of these was Joaquin, and the others were Reis and Valenzuela. The captive Mexican was hurried away to Cherokee Flat, where he was questioned closely in regard to his conduct. He played the part of an idiot, and would have succeeded in convincing the attendant crowd that he was really a poor imbecile, had he not been very well known by some of "the boys."

To bring him to his senses, hemp was suggested as a very efficacious thing in such cases, and he was accordingly elevated into the top of a tree to take a view of the surrounding country. The remedy operated upon his ailment like a charm, and he confessed without hesitation that he knew Joaquin, Reis, Valenzuela and numerous others of the banditti; and that Joaquin was at this time not far off, to whom he was taking provisions when he was apprehended.

A doubt arising in the minds of some persons, not noted for decision of character, as to whether it was right to put the fellow to death, Ellas left him in charge of the two Cherokee half-breeds, with the request that they would give a good account of him, whereupon the crowd dispersed. At about twelve o'clock in the night, the Cherokees went to Ellas' house in San Andreas, and informed him that they were ready to give "a good account" of the Mexican. Nothing more was said on the subject, and the next day he was found hanging on a tree by the side of the road.

Several weeks had now transpired since the fight on Chaparral Hill, and, notwithstanding the most diligent pursuit had been made after the robbers, yet during the whole time they had been busily engaged in murder, theft and plunder. They left a broad and bloody trail wherever they went, and committed their outrages at times in the very sight of their pursuers. Frequently were the harrowing cries of "murder" heard just ahead, and hurrying to the spot, citizens were found weltering in their blood, while the audacious bandits were seen riding off with no great evidence of fear at being overtaken. The banditti were divided the greater part of the time, into small companies of four or five, and Joaquin was seldom seen with more than three followers. Three-Fingered Jack was his constant attendant. Vulvia was in the field; Reis was active, and Valenzuela was far from idle.

On the 5th of February a Mexican was arrested by the citizen's at Angel's Camp. As soon as it was done, a young Sonorian gambler ran to a horse hitched at a rack, and was preparing to mount, no doubt to carry information to Joaquin of what had transpired, when a pistol was cocked in his face, and he was stopped. In a few moments it was ascertained that the man arrested was one of Joaquin's band and he soon made his exit into eternity, from the branch of an oak tree, which yet stands at Angel's Camp as one of its memorials.

Three or four Germans sleeping in a tent on a rather lonesome ravine, near to Angel's Creek, a few nights before the event last mentioned, were surprised to' find themselves suddenly tied hand and foot, in their beds, and still more horrified when a scowling band of ruffians stood over them with drawn sabres, which they drew across their throats so carelessly that it started the blood. The Germans eagerly delivered up what money they had, which amounted to the pitiful sum of two hundred dollars; at which Three-Fingered Jack, for he was there with his leader, jumped up with an oath that made the poor fellows quiver where they lay, and declared that he would dig their hearts out of them for not having any more, suiting his action to the word by brandishing his knife over their heads, and waving it to and fro within an inch of their windpipes. Joaquin, however, interfered and prevented him from executing his threat, remarking that it was better to let them live, as he might wish to collect taxes off them for "Foreign Miners' License," at some other time.

One Alexander Bidenger and his friend G. J. Mansfield, residing at a little place called Capulope, having learned from two friendly Mexicans that Joaquin had slept there on the night of the second of February, with other important information, concluded to send word to Justice Beatty the presiding magistrate at Campo Seco, not a great way off, and 'having written a letter despatched it by "Digger Express."

To those unacquainted with California customs, it may be necessary to explain that it is common in the mountains and mining districts to employ Digger Indians as bearers of letters, or runners upon errands, from one point to another, they being very expeditious on foot, and willing to travel a considerable distance for a small piece of bread, fresh meat or a ragged shirt. I have known them to swim rivers, when the waters were high and dangerous, in order to carry a letter to its destination. They are exceedingly faithful in this business, having a superstitious dread of that mysterious power which makes a paper talk without a mouth.

The naked expressman having been hunted up, he was charged by Bidenger to proceed to Campo Seco without delay, and to allow no one on the way to read the paper. The Digger, as is usual with these native expresses, got him a small stick about two feet long, and spliting the end to the depth of an inch or two, stuck the letter into it, and, holding it out in front of him, started off in a fast trot. One of Joaquin's party discovered him on the road, about three miles from Campo Seco, and wished to speak to him, but the Indian, remembering his charge, broke off at full speed, bearing the letter triumphantly before him. The robber fired two shots at the terrified native, which only accelerated his flight. Arriving at Campo Seco, he entered Beatty's office, and handed him the following unique epistle:

> February the 3, 1853
>
> I hereby gave notice that there is a thief and robber in this Capulope by the name of wakeen he slep here last night and he Is xpected to sleap heare tonight thar is not men enough here that will Assist in taking him he has horses tide back hear in the hills and six more men. i think it my duty to make it known.
>
> Alexander Bidenger and G. J. Mansfield.
> Rio Carrillo Bernardo Carasoo

The Justice having deciphered the hieroglyphical characters of this letter, as satisfactorily as he could, sent a messenger to the keepers of the ferry at Winter's Bar, to let no one cross during the night, believing that, from its proximity, that point would be selected by the robber for the passage of the river, in case he was closely pursued, and hurried off the Constable with a posse to rescue the six unfortunate men whom Joaquin had "tide" out in the hills. Arriving at Capulope in great heat, the Constable ascertained that there wore no six men tied out at all, but that the letter had designed to inform the Justice that Joaquin's party numbered six men.

"It's a pity," said Bidenger, "that a man of the Squire's larnin' can't read no better than that."

Nothing was seen of Joaquin in the neighborhood, though diligent search was made for him by the Constable from the time he left

Campo Seco until dark, but at midnight he rode up to the ferry at Winter's Bar, and requested to be set over. The keepers informed him that they had orders from the civil authorities to let no one pass, not even the Governor of the State, whereupon the impatient outlaw made such unequivocal, hostile demonstrations, that the ferrymen were glad to set aside the civil authorities, and for the time being, to obey martial law.

A few days after this, riding along with Three Fingered Jack, and another member named Pedro, Joaquin met two Americans and a German coming on foot from the direction of Murphy's Diggings, and bound for Australia, as their final destination. They were laden with gold dust, which they intended to convert into bills of exchange at San Francisco, and committed the great imprudence to run at the approach of the bandits, who, having been hotly pursued a few hours before by a party of citizens, might have passed on without harming them. Seeing them take flight, Joaquin said:

"Those fellows have money we must kill them."

The poor, terrified fugitives each took a separate course, and it was not long before they miserably perished under the murderous pistols and knives of the bandits. Dragging them by the heels, the robbers, who had secured their heavy purses, threw them into a hole which had been sunk by some prospectors, and covered them partially with leaves and bushes.

Riding on a little farther, upon a narrow pack-trail, which wound along on the bank of a foaming stream that was almost hid in the deep gorge through which it ran, they suddenly came upon a Chinese camp, containing six Chinamen. Though each had a double-barrelled shot-gun, they made no effort to defend themselves, but begged for their lives. Joaquin was disposed to spare them, but not wishing to leave his portrait impressed upon too many memories, which might prove some day quite too tenacious for his good, he concluded to kill Jack, by a nod from Joaquin, stepped as well as rob them. Three-Fingered up to each one, and led him out by his long tail of hair, repeating the ceremony until they all stood in a row before him.

He then tied their tails securely together, searched their pockets, while Pedro ransacked their tents, and, drawing his highly-prized home-made knife, commenced, amid the howling and shrieks of the unfortunate Asiatics, splitting their skulls and severing their neck veins. He was in his element, his eyes blazed, he shouted like a madman, and leaped from one to the other, hewing and cutting, as if it afforded him the most exquisite satisfaction to revel in human agony.

"Come," said Joaquin, "that's enough, mount up, and let's be off."

Reaching the main road again in a few hours they met the mail-rider between Jackson and Volcano, who, on perceiving them laid whip to his very fleet animal and narrowly escaped. Three-Fingered Jack on his fine black horse, could not in the whole race get nearer to him than fifty yards, and finally halted at that distance, and discharged three loads of his revolver at his slight figure, as he leaned forward with apparent anxiety to go faster than his horse was carrying him.

"By God," said Garcia, as he rode bank to Joaquin, "I would like to have caught that fellow, if nothing more than to get his horse. He flung dirt into my face faster than I ever saw it fly from a horse's heels before."

While laughing over the very exhilarating race which they had just had, a man named Horsely came insight, and was within one hundred yards of the brigands before he perceived them. Three-Fingered Jack's appearance was enough for him without any further examination, and wheeling his animal, a splendid bay mare, he proceeded to place as much ground as possible between himself and the dreaded party, which they on the other hand, undertook to diminish. Neck and heel they had it, for five miles, up the hills and down, Joaquin and Pedro a short distance behind, and the "Knight of the Three-Fingers" close on to the fugitive, who spared neither whip nor spur, at one time grasping at his bridle-rein, at another falling behind his horse's tail, and at another shooting at him with an unsuccessful aim.

Straggling travelers on the road, Jew peddlers, almond-eyed Chinamen, and deplorably ragged looking Frenchman, all, and everybody who happened to be on the road, gave way to the frantic rider and his head-long pursuers, gazing at them with unmitigated astonishment, and thanking their stars that they happened to be poor obscure foot-men. Horsely rode on, and on, and on, with unbated ardor on his own part, and no perceptible failure of vigor on the part of his horse, until within sight of a thickly populated mining district, when, giving him a farewell shot which rang in unpleasant proximity to his ear, Three-Fingered Jack roared out to him:

"You deserve to escape, old fellow, success to you!" and galloped back to his comrades, who had halted a few minutes before. "There's another fine horse," said he to his leader, "that we've missed getting."

Numerous murders having been committed, and many parties having failed to capture the leading desperadoes, an excitement prevailed, almost too intense to be borne, in the whole county of Calaveras.

About the 19th of February, a large meeting was held at the town of Jackson, at which it was resolved that everybody should turn out in search of the villain Joaquin. A committee of six men were secretly sent at midnight to Mokelumne Hill to secure a concert of action there, upon whose arrival, the citizens immediately assembled, and before morning two companies were organized, horse and foot, and placed under the command of Charles A. Clark, Esq., then Under Sheriff of the county.

Thus was the whole country alive with armed parties whose separate movements it would be impossible, without much unnecessary labor, to trace. Arrests were continually being made; popular tribunals established in the woods, Judge Lynch installed upon the bench; criminals arraigned, tried and executed upon the limb of a tree; pursuits, flights, skirmishes and a topsy-turvy, hurly-burly mass of events, that set narration at defiance. It remains only to give a few touches here and there, that an idea may be gathered of the exciting picture which the state of things then presented.

The Jackson Company went down on the west side of the Mokelumne River, while Clark directed his, companies to scour the woods and mountains in the direction of Campo Seco. From Campo Seco he went to Winter's Bar, crossed the river, and rode up to Stone & Baker's Rancho, where he met the Jackson Company. Learning that Joaquin had lately been seen at Camp Opera, the united parties surrounded that place about daylight, and huddled all the inhabitants, who were mostly Mexicans, together in a large tent, depriving them of their arms, and upon questioning them, ascertained that a Mexican horseman had come into town the day before and inquired of some women, who were washing at the branch near by, if they had seen Joaquin, and that he paid one of them fifty cents for washing a handkerchief deeply stained with blood.

Upon closer questioning, it appeared that the Mexican spoken of was himself present in the tent, and he was accordingly led forth for the especial consideration of his case. Finding that the trial to which they subjected him was no farce, and that they were actually going to hang him, he confessed that he was one of the brigands, and submitted with great composure to be choked to death. This was the end of the hitherto very lucky "Juan," for he seems never to have had a surname.

While their comrade was undergoing the penalty of death, Valenzuela and a few others, ignorant of the circumstance, were robbing a Dutchman only a few miles off, from whom they took six hundred dollars in beautiful specimens, for which the poor fellow had honestly labored six months in the mines. He was fortunate, however, in meeting with Valenzuela instead of Three-Fingered Jack, for he escaped with his life after a long debate between the robbers as to the propriety of letting him live, in which, the Dutchman afterwards acknowledged, he was more interested than in my question he had ever heard discussed.

Captain Ellas about this time heard of a suspicious fellow lurking around the little town or Camp of Los Muertos, and mounting his horse rode over to the tent in which he was harbored, and, with a pistol cocked in the villain's face, arrested him and took him to San Andreas. The people of that place appointed a Committee to investigate the case, and report their judgment as to what should be done in the premises. The Committee ascertained that he was wounded, a pistol ball having pierced him in such a manner as to make four different holes, from a twisted posture no doubt which he had assumed, and being able to elicit no satisfactory account as to how he had received the wound, they reported to the crowd that it was their opinion that it would not be amiss to hang him and risk it any how, whether he was guilty or not

Finding that he had to go, he confessed that he was the man whom Ellas had shot on Chaparral Hill, while he was endeavoring to catch his mare, and that he was with Joaquin when the two Americans, Peter Woodbeck and another were killed at the Phoenix Quartz Mill. The time-honored custom of choking a man to death was soon put into practice, and the robber stood on nothing kicking at empty space. Bah! it is a sight that I never like to see, although I have been civilized for a good many years.

On the 22d day of the month, one of the pursuing parties mentioned before, came upon five Mexicans, who were halted a few moments at a place called Forman's Camp, and immediately fired upon them, wounding one of them in the hand. Outnumbered, the robbers, among whom was the chief himself, rode off at full speed. The Americans followed, and had not proceeded far when pistol shots were heard in rapid succession at a, Chinese Camp at the foot of a hill upon which they were riding. Hastening down to the spot, they found three Chinamen dead, and five others writhing in their last agonies. The murderers were not more than ten minutes ahead. A dying Chinaman gasped out that they had been robbed of three thousand dollars.

Exasperated beyond measure at such audacity, the party rode furiously on in pursuit, but their horses had not the mettle to compete with those of the brigands, and they were forced to give it up for that day. On the 23d they resumed the pursuit, passing no less than a dozen Chinese camps which had been recently plundered, and towards evening caught sight of the rascals on the summit of a hill, engaged at the moment in knocking down some Chinamen, and robbing them. With a whoop of defiance, the daring chief led off his men before their faces, with such speed that they could not hope on their own scrub horses to overtake him.

The Chinese, beginning to believe that they were singled out for destruction, were seized with a general panic, and by the fifth of March might have been seen flocking from the mining districts in hundreds and thousands to the towns and cities. Mention the name of Joaquin to one of these Chinamen now, and his knees will quake like Belshazzar's.

Having ravaged the country for several long, and, to the people, distressing weeks, and having lost some of the bravest and most useful members of his band, and having aroused his enemies so that they met him on every trail, and surprised him at almost every encampment; having, besides this, collected by his plunders a large amount of money, Joaquin concluded to abandon Calaveras, and try his hand awhile on the citizens of Mariposa. Of course that county suffered, but it will not be necessary to recount anything like the entire series of his fearful deeds, in that devoted region, as it would only be a repetition of the bloody and harrowing scenes which have already sufficiently marked these pages.

His guardian fiend seemed never to desert him, and he came forth from every emergency in triumph. The following incident is but one among many, which shows the extraordinary success that attended him and would almost lead us to adopt the old Cherokee superstition, that there were some men who bear charmed lives, and whom nothing can kill but a silver bullet.

About the first of April in the little town of Hornitas, or Little Ovens, an American named Prescott, a very bold and resolute man, was one night informed by a friendly Mexican, who was a miner in that district, that Joaquin and four or five of his men were at that moment sleeping in a house kept by a Mexican woman, on the edge of the town.

"If I point him out to you," said he, be sure and kill him, for if you don't, my life is not worth three cents.

Prescott raised some fifteen men with secresy and despatch, and guided by the Mexican, gained the house without raising an alarm. Stationing his men around the house in every necessary direction, he and a few others cautiously entered. Candles were still burning, and everything was visible in the room.

"There they are," whispered the trembling Mexican, pointing to several heaps, rolled up in blankets, and slipping out as soon as he had spoken.

One of the party, holding a candle over Joaquin's face, in his anxiety to see if there might not possibly be a mistake, startled the formidable chief from his slumber, who, with a rapid return of consciousness, which belongs to men accustomed to danger, rose like lightning to his feet, cocking his pistol, as it were, in the very act of waking, and fired. The astonished candle holder staggered back, severely wounded in the side.

XIV

Combat Between Prescott and Joaquin—Robber Transactions in Yube County

Prescott, at the moment Joaquin fired at the candle holder, discharged both barrels of his shot-gun into the robber's breast, and was amazed to see him stand firm after a momentary stagger, and return the fire. Prescott very nearly fell to the floor, a ball having passed clean through his chest. The other bandits in the mean time having sprung up, blew out the lights, and firing their revolvers, shifted their positions, so that the Americans discharged their pistols into the space merely where their enemies had stood. Joaquin shot twice after the lights were extinguished, hitting a man each time, and with his pistol clubbed trode resolutely for the door.

Here he met an American, over whose head he shattered his pistol, very nearly killing him on the spot. It happened that at the same time that the bandits made their egress, a few Americans were also coming out, and before the two parties could be fairly separated, so as to render it safe to fire, the bold robbers had made their escape.

It is significant to add, that in a few days after this occurrence, the Mexican informer was found hanging to a tree, near the highway, his dead body bearing the marks of a recent terrible scourging. Joaquin was badly wounded by the discharge of Prescott's double-barreled shot-gun, and Three-Fingered Jack, who was now continually with him, was engaged—as he laughingly remarked to an acquaintance afterwards—for three weeks, off and on, in picking out buck-shot from his breast.

"How it come not' to kill him," said he, "the devil only knows, I'm certain it would have done the job for me."

But subsequent events will show that Jack himself was equally hard to kill. Prescott lay for a long time in a doubtful state, and Joaquin sent spies daily from his own sick-bed in the woods, to see if there was any prospect of his dying. Much to his disappointment Prescott recovered, and surely, after all he had suffered he is entitled to live a long time.

Valenzuela was at this time in the county of Yuba, in obedience to the order of his leader, who told him to do his best in the space of two weeks, and then to meet him at the Arroyo Cantoova rendezvous.

A description of one or two scenes which happened on Bear River, about twenty miles from the city of Marysville, will serve to give an idea of what he was about. This stream heads in the Sierra Nevada foot-hills, and crossing a broad plain empties into Feather River, near the town of Nicolaus. It waters, a fine agricultural and grazing region, and, houses, in the spring of 1853, as now, were scattered at intervals of four, five and six miles along its banks. In one of these houses lived an old widow woman, with her son and daughter.

These three, seated in their door on a pleasant evening, were surprised, as they lived off the public road, to see four huge fellows ride up, splendidly dressed, and armed to the teeth. One of them had four revolvers and a bowie knife. Dismounting, they requested supper. It was soon got in readiness by the brisk young lady—and she was as fresh and rosy a creature as ever one had the happiness to see—and the travelers partook of it most freely; the fellow with the four revolvers, who, notwithstanding his fierce look, was quite gentlemanly in his manners, conversing with her agreeably, as she politely waited upon them. The old woman looked rather suspiciously at the well-dressed eaters, from under her spectacles, but said nothing. As soon as they had finished, Valenzuela, for it was that worthy and none other, stepped up to where the young man was sitting, and cocking a pistol between his eyes, asked him if he had any objection to having the house robbed; if so, to name it. The old woman here screamed out:

"Oh Lord! I knowed it; I seed the cloven foot a stickin' out all the time," and continued to cry out with such vehemence that they were forced to put a gag, in her mouth. The young lady saved them the trouble of using that precaution in her case, by fainting.

The young man not relishing a cocked pistol in his face, with a man carelessly fingering the trigger, very readily gave his consent to have the house searched. Every drawer was ransacked, and every trunk burst open, and having obtained a few, hundred dollars, the robbers left.

At a late hour in the night another house was burst open, and the terrified inmates were dragged out of their beds, and securely bound hand and foot, besides being gagged, before they awoke sufficiently to know whether it was a dream or a reality. There was only one man at the house, the rest were women and children. All the money and jewelry was taken that could be found, and among other things, a gold watch, the chain of which Valenzuela very cooly put over his neck.

"Go to that old woman and take the gag out of her mouth," said he to one of his men, "she looks as if she were choking herself to death in the effort to say something."

As soon as the gag was removed, she begged Valenzuela with many tears, to give her back the watch, as it was a present from a dear friend, and contained a precious lock of hair.

"Certainly," said the robber, "if that's the case, I don't want it," and handed it to her.

Strange as it may seem at the first glance, the aged widow felt a sentiment of gratitude towards the robber, who, steeped in villainy as he was, had soul enough to answer an appeal of this kind. The unfortunate family were found the next morning by their neighbors, still lying upon the floor, bound hand and foot.

Such terror possessed that neighborhood for sometime afterwards that a traveler, no matter how peaceable his intentions, could no more get a chance to stay all night on that part of Bear River, than he could fly. A young fellow from the mountains, on his way down the valley, happening to be belated in that vicinity, called one night at every house in every direction, and was refused admittance, or hospitality, with an obstinacy which astonished him. The doors were barred on his approach, as if he had been a bearer of pestilence, and to his loud halloos and earnest solicitations for protection from the night air, he received the response that they had "no accommodation for travelers;" and he began to, believe that, indeed, they did have but little accommodation, sure enough.

It was drizzling rain, the hour was late, it was dark, and there were many deep and miry sloughs, which it was dangerous to pass unless in broad daylight. Directed at each refusal of "accommodation," to go to another house "jist acrost the slough," or "jist beyant that pint," the poor fellow wandered around nearly all night, narrowly escaping being drowned a dozen times, and finally, towards morning, leaving his horse tied on the bank of a slough and crossing to the other side in a canoe, he succeeded, after fighting a pitched battle with a gang of fierce dogs, in reaching an old shanty in a barley field, whose occupant, a bachelor, consented, to his great surprise, to let him stay. It seems the young fellow was dark-skinned, and unfortunately not very amiable looking fellow at best, and he was accordingly taken for Joaquin or some one of his band, traveling around as a spy.

XV

Advancing to a Close—State Legislature Taking Action to Protect the Country—Mounted Rangers Organized—Harry Love in Command—On Track Of the Bandits—Rangers Divide Into Two Companies

We come now near to the closing of the bandit's life; and, for the reason that unauthorized and fictitious accounts of the manner of his death, have been set float, I have taken very extraordinary pains in collecting and sifting the facts connected with that event, and the reader may rely upon the account given in these chapters as absolutely correct in every particular.

So burdensome were the tributes levied upon the citizens, that it became a fit subject for Legislative action. The officers of the law in the different counties were either shot down in cold blood or openly defied by the bandits. The constant arming of private companies for the protection of the lives and property of citizens was become too extensive a drain upon the pockets of private individuals. In many agricultural districts both mining and agricultural pursuits were in a measure suspended. Travel became absolutely dangerous in the most open highways, and communication had well nigh ceased between important points.

Women and children in lonely places, suffering from constant fear, were often removed to more thickly populated localities, with great trouble and at heavy expense. American owners of ranches were impoverished in a night by having every hoof of their stock driven into the mountains, and afterward into Sonora. The condition of things, in short, became intolerable, and a petition, numerously signed, was presented to the Legislature praying that body to authorize Captain Harry Love to organize a company of Mounted Rangers, in order to capture, or drive out of the country, or exterminate the highwaymen.

A bill to this effect was passed, signed by the Governor on the 17th of May, 1853, and a company organized by Harry Love on the 28th of the same month. The pay was set down at one hundred and fifty dollars per month per man, and the legal existence of the company limited to three months, while the number of men was not to exceed twenty, the object being to surprise and take, or kill, Joaquin, in some one of the numerous expeditions in which he was in the habit of engaging, accompanied, for convenience sake, and purposes of greater secrecy, by small bodies of men.

Notwithstanding the slender amount of wages allowed, each member was required to furnish his own horse, provisions and equipments, at his individual expense.

Without hesitation, may, with alacrity, for it was in consonance with his daring spirit, Love immediately took the command of twenty choice men, selected for their well-known courage, and led them forth to meet as formidable a man as ever figured in the arena of crime. The following is a list of their names: P. E. Connor, C. F. Bloodworth, G. W. Evans, Wm. Byrnes, John Nuttal, Wm. S. Henderson, C. V. McGowan, Robert Masters, W. H. Harvey, George A. Nuttal, Col. McLane, Lafayette Black, D. S. Hollister, P. T. Herbert, John S. White, Willis Prescott, James M. Norton, Coho Young, E. B. Van Dorn and S. K. Piggott.

Several of the names in the foregoing list will be recognized as those of men already prominent in, the counties in which they lived, and afterwards occupying positions of more or less distinction in the State. One of them represented California for two years in the Lower House in the United States Congress, and became involved in a serious difficulty at Washington, in which he drew a derringer and killed an Irish waiter at one of the hotels, who had Tor some reason or other attacked him. The affray was variously represented by the partisan prints of the day, some justifying the act of the California member, and others denouncing it as a cold-blooded murder. At any rate, Mr. Herbert was tried and acquitted.

This brave but small party of Mounted Rangers were looked upon by the anxious eyes of the community, from whose midst they started, as almost certainly destined to destruction. But they forgot that a leader was now in the field, and armed with the authority of the State, whose experience was a part of the stormiest histories of the frontier settlements, the civil commotions of Texas, and the stirring events of the Mexican War; whose soul was as rugged and severe as the discipline through which it had passed; whose brain was as strong and clear in the midst of dangers, as that of the daring robber against whom he was sent and who possessed a glance as quick, and a hand as sudden in the execution of a deadly purpose.

With untiring energy, and most stealthy movements, Captain Love set himself to work to obtain a full knowledge of the haunts of the bandit chief, the latest traces of his steps, and all that was necessary to enable him to fall upon him at the best possible time and place. While on this lookout for him, Joaquin was busy in making his preparations for the grand finale of his career in California. After robbing extensively on the Little Mariposa, and the Merced River, he proceeded to the rancho of Joaquin Guerra, near to San' Jose, killing a Frenchman on his way, who kept the Tivola Gardens, and there stopped for a few weeks, lying concealed. The *Major Domo* of this rancho, Francisco Sicarro, was secretly connected with his band, and this accounts for his staying there.

In the meantime he had despatched Luis Vulvia to the Arroyo Cantoova, with orders to remove the women to a place of safety in the province of Sonora; to send Valenzuela, as soon as he, should arrive at the rendezvous, to the same State with remittances of money, and with instructions to arm and equip his followers and adherents there, who stood in waiting, and to proceed himself to the different harboring ranchos in California, and collect at the Arroya Cantoova all the horses which had been left upon them from time to time. It was his own intention to go to the rendezvous in a short time and wait for the arrival of his forces. The extreme caution with which this wily leader was bringing his plans to a focus, is aptly exhibited in the following comparative little incident.

Feeling one evening somewhat inclined for a dram, and unwilling to show his own person, he sent from Guerra's rancho an Indian, to bring him a bottle of liquor from San Jose. After the Digger had started, he became a little uneasy lest the fellow should betray him, and mounting his horse, overtook him on the road to Coyote Creek, and killed him.

On the first day of July, seventy of his followers had arrived at the Arroyo Cantoova, with fifteen hundred horses, and in another part of the valley, Joaquin himself, with Reis, Three-Fingered Jack, and a few other men were waiting for the final arrival of all his forces from Sonora and other quarters. His correspondence was large with many wealthy and influential Mexicans residing in the State of California, and he had received assurances of their earnest co-operation in the movement which he contemplated. A shell was about to burst, which was little dreamed of by the mass of the people who merely looked upon Joaquin as the petty leader of a band of cut throats!

XVI

Captain Love With Only Eight Men Comes Upon the Encampment of Joaquin—Remarkable Coolness of the Bandit—Desperate Leap on Horseback—Death of Three-Fingered Jack—Subsequent Movement of Rangers—Conclusion

On the fifth of July, Captain Love, who had been secretly tracing the bandit in his movements, left with his company the town of San Jose and camped near San Juan for four or five days, scouring the mountains in that vicinity. From San Juan he started in the night, on the coast route, in the direction of Los Angeles, and tarried a night or two on the Salinas Plains. Thence he went across the San Bonita Valley, camping just before daylight, without being discovered by any one, in a small valley in the coast range, near to Quien Sabe Rancho. Leaving this place, after a short survey of the neighborhood, he proceeded to the Eagle's Pass, and there came upon a party of Mexicans, who were going, or said so at least, in the Tulares to capture the wild mustangs, which fed there in great numbers.

From this point the Rangers divided, a portion going to the Chico Panoche Pass, and the others taking a course through the mountains. They found trails which led both divisions to the same point, that is, to the Bayou Seetas, or Little Prairie. Before reaching this point Love stopped a few Mexicans, who were evidently carrying forward the news of his advance into that wild and suspicious region. Separating again, the company again met at the Grand Panoche Pass, from which they went on in a body to the Arroyo Cantoova. Here they found the seventy or eighty men, of Joaquin's band, spoken of above, with the fifteen hundred stolen horses.

These men, it would be fair to infer, could have annihilated the small party of twenty men opposed to them, had they seen fit, and it was a wise act in Captain Love to deceive them as he did, by informing them that he was executing a commission on the part of the State to obtain a list of all the names of those who were engaged in mustang hunting, in order that a tax might be collected from them for the privilege, in accordance with a late act of the Legislature. With this explanation, and going through the farce of taking down a list of their names, which were no doubt fictitious, every one of them, he started on in the direction of San Juan, but turned about seven or eight miles off, at the head of the Arroyo, in order to watch their movements.

It was now the 24th of the month, on the morning of which day he went back to their encampment, and found it wholly deserted, not a man or horse left. Fully convinced from this sudden abandonment of the place, that, they were nothing less than a portion of Joaquin's band, he resolved to follow their trail. On the 25th, which was Sunday, at three o'clock in the morning, he reached the Tulare Plains, where he found they had parted their company—some going south towards the Tejon Pass, and others north towards the San Joaquin River. Detailing a portion of the Rangers to proceed to Mariposa county with some stolen horses which had been recovered on the way, the Captain, with the remainder of his party, numbering only eight men, dauntlessly pursued the southern trail, which led in the more proper direction for finding Joaquin.

Just at daylight he saw a smoke rising from the plains on his left, and wishing to allow no circumstance, however trivial, to pass unnoticed, at a time so much requiring his utmost vigilance, he turned from the trail and rode out towards it. He saw nothing more than some loose horses, until within six hundred yards of the spot from which the smoke proceeded, when rising a mound, he discovered seven men scattered around a small fire, one of whom was a few steps off, washing a fine looking bay horse with water which he held in a pan. Their sentinel, who had just been cooking, at this moment caught sight of the approaching party, and gave the alarm to his comrades, who all rushed forth in the direction of their horses, except the man who already held his by the lariat at camp. Dashing up in hot haste, the Rangers succeeded in stopping every man before he got to his animal.

The Captain, riding up to the individual who stood holding the horse, questioned him as to the course upon which he and the others were traveling. He answered that they were going to Los Angeles. Giving the nod to two of his young men, Henderson and White, they stood watching this individual, while the Captain rode toward others of the suspicious looking party, who, I have omitted to say, were all Mexicans, superbly dressed, each wearing over their finery a costly broadcloth cloak. Addressing one of these others in relation to their destination, he replied in direct contradiction to what the other had just said, who, flushing up with an angered look, exclaimed:

"No! we're going to Los Angeles;" and turning to Love, said: "Sir, if you have any questions to ask, address yourself to me. I am the leader of this company."

Love answered, "that he would address himself to whom he pleased, without consulting him."

The leader, as he called himself, then advanced a few steps towards the saddles and blankets, which lay around the fire, when Love told him to stop. He walked on without heeding the command, when the Captain drew his six-shooter, and told him if he did not stop in an instant he would blow his brains out. With a proud toss of his head, and grating his teeth together in rage, he stepped back and laid his hand again upon his horse's mane, which had stood quietly during the moment he was away. This individual was Joaquín Murieta, though Love was ignorant of the fact. He was armed only with a bowie-knife, and was advancing towards his saddle to get his pistols at the time Love covered him with his revolver.

A short distance off stood Three-Fingered Jack, fully armed and anxiously watching every movement of his chief. Separated by the Rangers, surprised, and unable to act in concert; on foot, and unable to get to their horses, were scattered here and there others of the party. The danger to Joaquin was great and imminent, yet no sign of fear played upon his countenance. He held his head firmly, and looked around him with a cool and unflinching glance, as if he calmly studied the desperate chances of the time. He patted, from time to time, his horse upon the neck, and the fiery steed raised his graceful head pricked up his sharply pointed ears, and stood with flashing eyes, as if ready to spring at a moment's warning.

Lieut. Byrnes, who had known the young robber when he was an honest man, a few years before, soon rode into camp, having fallen behind by order of the captain, and immediately on his approach, Joaquin, who knew him at the first sight, called out to his followers to make their escape, every man for himself. Three-Fingered Jack bounded off like a mighty stag of the forest. He was shot at by several of the Rangers, and attention being momentarily called away from Joaquin, he mounted his fine bay horse, already eager to run, and rode off, without saddle or briddle, at the speed of the wind. A dozen balls from the Colt's repeaters whizzed by him without effect. Rushing along a rough and rocky ravine, with that recklessness that belongs to a bold rider and a powerful, high-spirited animal, he leaped from a precipice ten or twelve feet high, and was thrown violently from his horse, which turned a half somersault as he touched the ground and fell on his back with his heels within a few inches of his master's head. Horse and rider recovering themselves in a moment, Joaquin again, mounted with the quickness of lightning, and was again on the wing. One of his pursuers, named Henderson, fearlessly leaped after him, while others who were not so close behind, galloped around to head him at a certain favorable point.

Henderson and horse went through the same tumbling motions as in the example which had preceded him. He was not mounted so soon but that Joaquin was some distance ahead before he was fairly E ready to renew the chase. The bold chieftain was fast escaping danger on his swift and beautiful steed, and a few more vigorous bounds would carry him beyond the reach of gun-shot, when one of the pursuing party, finding that they could not hit the rider, levelled his rifle at the horse, and sent a ball obliquely into his side. The noble animal sunk a moment, but rose again, still vigorous, though bleeding, and was bearing his master as if he knew his life depended upon *him*, clearly out of all reach of a bullet or any fear of a capture, when alas!

For the too exulting hopes of the youthful chieftain, the poor beast, with a sudden gush of blood from his mouth and nostrils, fell dead beneath him. A fortunate shot, whoever aimed that rifle! Joaquin, now far ahead of his pursuers, ran on, on foot. They outran him upon their horses, and coming again within pistol-shot discharged several balls into his body. When the third ball struck him, he turned around facing them, and said:

"Don't shoot any more—the work is done!"

He stood still a few moments, turning pale as his life-blood ebbed away, and sinking slowly to the ground upon his right arm, surrendered to death.

While their beloved leader was proudly submitting to the inexorable Fate which fell upon him, if we may call it Fate, when it was born from his own extreme carelessness in separating himself from the main body of his men, and in a habitual feeling of too much security at his rendezvous, his followers were struggling for their lives against fearful odds in all directions over the plains.

Three-Fingered Jack, pursued by Love himself and one or two others, ran five miles before he fell, pierced with nine balls. He leaped over the ground like a wild beast of the chase, and frequently gained a considerable distance on his pursuers, whose horses would sometimes stumble in the gopher holes, and soft soil of the plain, and throw their riders headlong in the dirt. When overtaken, he would wheel with glaring eyes and with a whoop of defiance, discharge his six-shooter.

Though a good shot, out of five trials he missed every time. Circumstances were against him, but he was determined never to be taken alive, and to no proposal to surrender would he listen a moment, but ran on as long as his strength would sustain him, and fought till he fell, dying with his hand on his pistol, which he had emptied of every load but one. He was at last shot through the head by Captain Love, who had wounded him twice before in the long chase. Three-Fingered Jack, anomalous as it may seem to be, while he was the very incarnation of cruelty, was at the same time as brave a man as this world ever has produced, and so died, as those who killed him will testify.

Shortly after the chase of Joaquin and Three-Fingered Jack commenced, three of the band not before discovered, galloped out into the plain from a point a little below Joaquin's camp fire where they had probably made a small separate encampment the night before, and dismounted in full view of several of the Rangers, who approached them on three sides. They stood still until within reach of pistol shot, when they suddenly sprang into their saddles, and firing their revolvers at the approaching Rangers, rode off. The Rangers returned the fire with effect, wounding two of the men and one of the horses. Their animals being remarkably swift, they distanced their pursuers, and reached the foot of the mountains without further injury.

But just at this point one of the wounded men grew so faint that he fell back in the flight, and a comrade falling a back also, to assist him, thus gave the Rangers an opportunity to come within s gunshot. As he galloped off with his s wounded companion to rejoin his brothers ahead, a skillful marksman levelled a rifle at his retreating figure and sent a ball into his back that made him reel upon his horse, and thus added one more to the wounded list, which now comprised the whole party. They succeeded in escaping, but one of them fell from his horse during the following night and died in a solitary place among the mountains.

The pursuit being ended on all parts of the field, the Rangers returned to the point from which they had started. As yet, all were ignorant of the true character of the party which they had attacked. Byrnes did not happen to be looking at Joaquin when he first rode into camp, and consequently had not recognized him at all, not being with the individuals who succeeded in killing him. When they all got together it was ascertained that four Mexicans had been killed and two others taken prisoners. Going up to the dead bodies, one was immediately recognized by Byrnes as that of Joaquín Murieta, and another, by some one else, as that of Three-Fingered Jack.

It was important to prove to the satisfaction of the public that the famous and bloody bandit was actually killed, else the fact would be eternally doubted, and many unworthy suspicions would attach to Captain Love. He accordingly acted as he would not otherwise have done; and I must shock the nerves of the fastidious, much against my will, by stating that he caused the head of the renowned Murieta to be cut off, and to be hurried away with the utmost expedition to the nearest place, one hundred and fifty miles, at which any alcohol could be obtained in which to preserve it.

Three-Fingered Jack's head was also cut off, but being shot through soon became offensive, and was thrown away. His hand, however, was preserved—that terrible three-fingered hand, which had dyed itself in many a quivering heart, had torn with its talons the throats of many an agonized victim, and had shadowed itself forth upon the horrified imaginations of thousands who only knew that it existed.

The head, which for a long time retained a very natural appearance, was thoroughly identified in, a every quarter where its owner was known.

The hand was also exhibited in a glass case, not to prove its identity, though even that was done, but to give the public the actual sight of an object which had flung a strange, haunting dread over the mind, as if it had been a conscious voluntary agent of evil.

Many superstitious persons, ignorant of the phenomenon which death presents in the growth of the hair and nails, were seized with a kind of terror to observe that the moustache of the fearful robber had grown longer since his head had been cut off, and that the nails of Three-Fingered Jack's hand had lengthened almost an inch.

The bloody encounter being over, Love gathered up the spoils, which consisted of seven fine animals, which were afterwards restored to their owners, six elegant Mexican saddles and bridles, six Colt's revolvers, a brace of holster pistols, and five or six pairs of spurs. Three splendid horses were killed under their riders in the chase. Five or six fine broadcloth cloaks were found at the camp. Money, there was none. One of the prisoners, however, declared that Three-Fingered Jack, during the chase, threw away a very large purse of gold, which was encumbering him in his flight; and it is probable that others did the same.

Upon the return of the Rangers from this expedition one of the prisoners, after vainly endeavoring to persuade his companion to follow his example, suddenly broke loose from his captors, and plunging into a deep slough near by, bravely drowned himself. The other was taken to Mariposa county jail, and there confined until the company were ready to disband, when he was transferred to Martinez.

While there he made a confession, implicating a large number of his countrymen in the villainies which had been perpetrated, and was prepared to make still more important disclosures perhaps with the view of making the value of his information weigh against his execution—when he was forestalled in a mysterious manner. The jail was broken open one night at the dead hours, and the prisoner taken out by an armed mob and hung. The Americans knew nothing of the hanging, so that the most rational conjecture is that he was put out of the way by Mexicans, to prevent the damning revelations which he certainly would have made.

Among the numerous affidavits identifying the robber's head, the reader may take the following as specimens of the remainder. The Reverend Father Dominie Blaine, who knew Joaquin well, and who had often confessed wounded members of his band, testified as follows:

> State Of California,
> County of San Joaquin,
>
> On this, the 11th day of August, 1853, personally came before me, A. C. Baine, a Justice of the Peace in and for said county, the Reverend Father Dominie Blaine, who makes oath, in due form of law, that he was acquainted with the notorious robber, Joaquin; that he has just examined the captive's head, now in the possession of Captain Connor, of Harry Love's Rangers, and that he verily believes the said head to be that of the individual Joaquín Murieta, so known by him two years ago, as before stated.
>
> D. Blaine
>
> Sworn to and subscribed before me the day and year aforesaid.
>
> A. C. Baine, J. P.

Ignacio Lisarrago, of Sonora, well known in the lower part of the State as follows:

> State Of California,
> City and County of San Francisco
>
> Ignacio Lisarrago, of Sonora, being duly sworn, says: That he has seen the alleged head of Joaquin, now in the possession of Messrs. Nutall and Black, two of Captain Love's Rangers, on exhibition at the saloon of John King, Sansome Street. That deponent was well acquainted with Joaquín Murieta and that the head so exhibited is and was the veritable head of Joaquín Murieta, the celebrated bandit.
>
> Ignacio Lisarrago
>
> Sworn to before me, this 17th day of August, 1853.
>
> Charles D. Carter,
> Notary Public

Affidavits like these, together with certificates from sworn officers of the law, and the voluntary verbal testimony of hundreds of visitors at the different exhibitions were more than sufficient to satisfy the legal authorities of the death of the noted chieftain.

Accordingly the Governor of the State, John Bigler, caused to be paid to Captain Love the sum of one thousand dollars, which in his official capacity he had offered for the capture of the bandit, dead or alive.

And subsequently, on the 15th day of May, 1854, the Legislature of California, considering that his truly valuable services in ridding the country of so great a terror were not sufficiently rewarded, passed an act granting him an additional sum of five thousand dollars.

The story is told.

Briefly, and without the aid of ornament, the life and character of Joaquín Murieta have been sketched. His career was short, for he died in his twenty-second year; but in the few years which were allowed him, he displayed qualities of mind and heart which marked him an extraordinary man, and leaving his name impressed upon the early history of this State, he also leaves behind him the important lesson that there is nothing so dangerous in its consequences as *injustice to individuals*—whether it arise from prejudice of color or any other source; that a wrong done to one man is a wrong to society and to the world.

It is only necessary to add, that after the death of its chief, the mighty organization which he had established was broken up. It exists now only in scattered fragments over California and Mexico. Its subordinate chiefs—among whom is the yet living Valenzuela—lacking the brilliancy and unconquerable will of their leader, will never be able to revive it in its full force; and although all the elements are still in active existence, they will make themselves felt in nothing more, it is probable, than petty outbreaks here and there, and depredations of such a character as can easily be checked by the vigilance of the laws.

Of Rosita, the beautiful and well-beloved of Joaquin, the writer knows no further than that she remains in the Province of Sonora, silently and sadly working out the slow task of a life forever blighted to, her, under the roof of the parents of her dead lover.

Alas!

How happy might she not have been had man never learned to wrong his fellow man!

A Note About the Author

John Rollin Ridge (1827–1867) was a novelist, poet, and member of the Cherokee Nation. Born in New Echota Georgia, Ridge was the son of John Ridge, a prominent Cherokee leader and signatory of the 1836 Treaty of New Echota, which allowed the cession of Cherokee lands and led to the devastation of the Trail of Tears. Following his father's murder by supporters of Cherokee leader John Ross, Ridge was taken to Arkansas by his mother. In 1843, he was sent to study at the Great Barrington School in Massachusetts before returning to Fayetteville to pursue a law degree. He married Elizabeth Wilson in 1847 after publishing his first known poem, "To a Thunder Cloud," in the *Arkansas State Gazette*. Two years later, Ridge was forced to flee to California with his wife and daughter after murdering a man named David Kell, whom he believed to be involved in his father's assassination. Out West, he published *The Life and Adventures of Joaquín Murieta* to popular acclaim, making him the first known Native American novelist. Ridge was a prominent figure in California's fledgling literary scene, serving as the first editor of the *Sacramento Bee* and writing for the *San Francisco Herald*. Controversial for his assimilationist politics, slave ownership, and support of the Copperheads during the American Civil War, Ridge is nevertheless a pioneering figure in Native American literary history.

A Note from the Publisher

Printed in the USA
CPSIA information can be obtained
at www.ICGtesting.com
JSHW021454180324
59436JS00007B/151

9 781513 283418